CHRISTMAS IN THE KING'S BED

CAITLIN CREWS

MILLS & BOON

First published in Great Britain 2020
by Mills & Boon, an imprint of HarperCollins*Publishers*
1 London Bridge Street, London, SE1 9GF

Large Print edition 2021

© 2020 Caitlin Crews

ISBN: 978-0-263-28827-8

MIX
Paper from
responsible sources
FSC
www.fsc.org
FSC™ C007454

This book is produced from independently certified FSC™ paper to ensure responsible forest management. For more information visit www.harpercollins.co.uk/green.

Printed and bound in Great Britain
by CPI Group (UK) Ltd, Croydon, CR0 4YY

WA

CHRISTMAS IN
THE KING'S BED

CHAPTER ONE

"YOUR BETROTHED IS waiting for you, sire," came the diffident voice of King Orion's personal steward from behind him. "In your private salon, as requested."

Orion murmured his thanks, but didn't turn around. He kept his brooding gaze on his beloved country, laid out before him in the November sun. This view from the heights of the palace took in the largest town on the main island that made up the kingdom of Idylla, a sweep of stark-white buildings with the blue Aegean beyond. He had always loved this view. In the long, dark days of his father's tumultuous, dissolute reign—meaning, the whole of Orion's life until a few months ago—he had often stood here. He had gazed out on the splendor of the tiny kingdom that had endured so many wars, regime changes, and horrors in its time, yet still stood.

He had told himself that Idylla would survive his father, too.

And he had spent long hours imagining what he would do differently when it was his turn to rule. How best he could honor and serve his people, who deserved so much better than what they'd had in King Max.

Orion had vowed he would do whatever it took to erase his people's memories of his father's excesses and scandals. Whatever it took to restore peace and serenity to the island kingdom.

But now the time had come to do just that.

And he did not want any part of it.

"'Your betrothed,'" echoed his brother, Prince Griffin, in the lazily sardonic tone that matched the way he lounged in his preferred armchair, there before the fireplace that took up the better part of one wall. "You do know that you're the king now, Orion—don't you? I was there when they put the crown on your head."

"Do you mean when you swore an oath of fealty to me?" Orion asked mildly, without turning around. "Feel free to enact it."

"Yes, yes, my entire life is an act of homage

to my liege," Griffin murmured in the same tone. He paused a moment. "You could also choose *not* to be betrothed. Then make it law. Again—you are the king. You can do as you like. I would have thought that was the main benefit of the whole thing."

Orion could do just that. Of course he could. But there were factors at play that Griffin didn't know about and, more important, Orion had given his word. Their father had gone back on his word habitually. Constantly. King Max's word had been meaningless.

Orion had no intention of being anything like his father.

"If I did such a thing I would be no better than him," he said quietly, to the only other person alive who knew how seriously he took these things.

"You were born better than him," Griffin retorted, a familiar harshness in his voice that always accompanied any discussion of their late, unlamented father.

Because King Max had not simply been a bad monarch, though he was that. In spades. He had been a far worse father than he'd been a king, and a terrible husband to their mother to boot.

But this was not the time to compare scars.

The future Orion had promised his people was here. He was that future. And he had no intention of breaking his promises. His earliest memories were of the vows his father had broken, one after the next, as if it was a game to him. He had betrayed his family and his country with the same carelessness. Orion would do neither.

No matter how little he liked what he needed to do next.

When he'd been sixteen, he had made a vow to the pack of reporters who had followed him about, clamoring for the crown prince's take on his father's every scandal. He had told them with all the ringing intensity of youth that *he* would live a blameless, honorable, scandal-free life.

Orion had gone to extraordinary lengths to keep that promise.

He saw no reason to stop now.

"Then I will leave you to your martyrdom," his younger brother said. "I know how you love it."

Orion turned, then. Griffin grinned at him, then rose—as wholly unrepentant as ever. He stretched like a cat instead of a prince, because he had always taken great pleasure in flaunting his physicality at every turn.

The spare could do as he liked. The heir, on the other hand, had always to think first of the kingdom.

Their father had apparently missed that lesson, but Orion had stamped it deep into his bones.

"Duty comes for us all, brother," he said lightly.

Or lightly for him, in any case.

"I haven't forgotten what I promised you," Griffin replied. "Even though, obviously, you could wave your autocratic pinkie and save us both from our fates." He let out a long, delighted laugh when Orion only frowned at him. "Please spare me another lecture on what we owe our subjects. Or your subjects, more like. I've heard it all before. I, too, will commit myself to blamelessness. Soon."

"It becomes no less true in the retelling," Orion said with what he hoped was quiet dignity. Instead of what he actually felt. That being the lowering realization that if he could, he would shirk this betrothal in a heartbeat, no matter what destruction that might cause. He would wave the royal pinkie—

But he did not break vows. To himself, to others, or to his people.

That had to be the beginning and the end of it, or who was he?

Griffin rolled his eyes at his older brother and king as if he could read Orion's mind. He likely could. He lifted a hand, then prowled his way out of Orion's private office. No doubt off to despoil virgins, carouse, and enjoy the last days of the scandalous reputation he'd built for himself as possibly the most unrepentant playboy in the history of Europe.

Orion stood where he was, a muscle in his jaw flexing with a tension and fury he couldn't control.

You are *controlling it,* he told himself stoutly. *Because, unlike your father, you are always in control. Always.*

And always, always would be. That was one more promise he'd made himself.

He blew out a breath, there where even Griffin couldn't see him.

And then there was nothing for it. Putting off his unpleasant duty wasn't going to make it any better. It wasn't going to save him from the unwelcome task he had no choice but to perform.

Like everything else in his life, he was simply going to have to do what must be done, no matter what.

His personal feelings were irrelevant and always had been.

He had learned that beyond any reasonable doubt when, at seventeen, he'd been the one to discover his mother, the queen, after she'd taken her own life. And when his father had proved unequal to the task of handling her funeral—preferring to decamp to the Caribbean with a brace of starlets on each arm—Orion had stepped in to handle it.

Not because he'd wanted to handle it. He'd been seventeen. Still considered a child by some. But despite his feelings and his youth, he'd handled it because it needed to be handled.

As the years passed, his father had increased his vile behavior, made ever more unhinged demands, and had shirked more and more of his royal duties. Orion had stepped in and shouldered the load, each and every time.

He'd been doing the lion's share of the monarch's actual work for a decade, but always with the knowledge that at any moment, on the slightest whim, his father could and likely would sweep in and undo all his work.

Today was an example of the old king's machinations from beyond the grave, in point of fact, and it was the same as it ever had been. As if he was still alive to ruin lives. Orion would have to do what needed doing, not because he *wanted* to do it. But because it was for the good of Idylla.

He pushed away from the window and headed for his door, automatically checking his appearance in one of the mirrors as he passed. Not because he was vain, but because he was the crown. And in contrast to his father's visible, heedless decline, he wished to look above reproach—and as much like the official photographs of himself—as possible.

Because that helped his people feel secure.

Everything Orion did was to make Idylla better. To convince his people that all was well, that he could be trusted, that the years of shame and scandal were behind them all. Part of that was presenting them with an image of a king they could believe in.

One that was as opposite his father's slovenly appearance in his last years as possible.

Orion looked presentable enough, and left his office, moving swiftly now that he'd stopped stalling the inevitable.

He might not wish to be betrothed, but he was. And that meant he was getting married, because a broken betrothal was a broken promise—a scandal in the making—and he would allow neither.

No matter what happened.

The palace corridor outside his office was quieter than it had been while his father was alive, when Orion's staff had always rushed to and fro, always in one crisis or another as they'd all done their best to anticipate and/or manage the king's mercurial decisions. Becoming king had actually eased Orion's duties in many ways, because he no longer had to spend 89 percent of his time conjuring up ways to handle the fallout of each and every one of King Max's contradictory decrees.

Competent, reserved, and sane. Those were Orion's goals as king.

Idylla had been the world's punch line for far too long. It ended now.

His betrothed might not know it yet, she might have her own agenda, for all he knew— but despite who she was and what she represented, she would fall in line with the goals of his new regime.

One way or the other.

Or she would pay the price.

He headed toward his private salon, nodding at courtiers and staff as he went. No one approached him, which told him he probably ought to do something about his expression.

But he didn't.

Because he was not his brother, who could produce a smile from the ether on command, then wield it like a weapon. Orion had not spent years perfecting a *smile*, thank you, when he'd had a kingdom to run and a rogue monarch to manage. His face did what it would.

He opened the door to his private salon briskly, prepared to lay out his plans and his expectations—

But the room was empty.

Orion blinked. He prided himself on being approachable, and no particular stickler for courtly etiquette, but he was still the king. Even as the crown prince, there was only one person who had ever dared keep him waiting—and his father was dead.

This was not an auspicious beginning to matrimonial life.

A moment later he realized the French doors that opened out onto one of the balconies was ajar. He frowned, because this was not part of his plan. Moreover, he would have laid odds—not that he ever gambled the way his father had—that his betrothed would have been eager for this meeting he'd been putting off for the better part of two years. He wouldn't have been surprised if she'd stood just inside the door, waving one of her father's tabloids in his face while crowing about her victory and his capitulation.

He'd expected as much, in fact.

And perhaps that wasn't fair, he thought, because he prided himself on fairness, too. Or tried. The truth was, he knew very little about Lady Calista Skyros, the woman he was meant to marry. Because no matter what he liked to thunder at his brother, he too had been holding out hope that he wouldn't have to do this.

Lady Calista was the eldest daughter of perhaps the single most vile citizen of the kingdom of Idylla, now the old king was dead. Aristotle Skyros had been born into Idyllian nobility, had ponced about in between various universities—getting sent down from each in turn—and had blown through his own fortune by the age of twenty-three. Luckily for him, his appalled father had died shortly thereafter, with no choice but to leave his considerable estate in his disappointing son's hands. According to the many interviews he gave on his favorite topic—himself—Aristotle had disliked the seven months of so-called destitution he'd experienced and had thus vowed to do better with his second fortune.

Annoyingly, he had. He now owned a sprawling media empire, almost entirely made up of the kind of tabloid filth that made anyone who looked at it dirty. And those who were featured against their will in his snide, insinuating columns and slickly produced shows could never make themselves clean again.

As Orion knew personally.

When his father had announced, three years ago, that he had arranged Orion's eventual marriage, Orion had not bothered to argue about it. There was no point fighting his father, especially not when the old king was deep in his cups, which was where he'd preferred to live. Orion had assumed that if he waited it out, his father would reverse himself. Possibly within the hour—another thing that happened with alarming regularity.

But instead, his father had died. In the squalid circumstances the country and the world had come to expect from him, naturally, with unfortunate women and mood-altering substances all around. Because why change in death what he had so exulted in during his life?

Aristotle Skyros had slithered out of his hellhole and into the palace almost before *"The king is dead, long live the king"* finished echoing through the halls. And he had made it known that as far as he was concerned, the betrothal the old king had made between the new King of Idylla and his daughter was set in stone.

"Surely I decide what is stone and what is nothing more than a bad dream we have now happily woken up from," Orion had said.

With perhaps more menace than was wise.

Aristotle, an unpleasantly dissipated-looking man whose bald head gleamed with the same malevolence that was apparent in his gaze, had smiled. Oily and insincere.

"You can do anything you please, Your Majesty," he had replied unctuously. He'd bowed his head as if in deference. "As will I, if necessary."

Orion had been tempted to pretend he didn't recognize the threat in the other man's words. He had been king for a matter of hours at that point, and had been naive enough to imagine there might be some kind of grace period. Some allowance while he found his feet—but no. Of course not.

But he had tamped down on his temper and had not, sadly, strangled the other man where he sat. "If you wish to threaten me, Skyros, I suggest you do it. I detest pretense."

Aristotle had not bothered with another show of false obeisance. "You will marry my daughter, Majesty. Because if you do not, I will have no choice but to release a selection of photographs I have in my possession that were in a private collection for years. Photographs so shocking and potentially explosive that your father offered you as collateral to keep them hidden."

Orion had scoffed at that. "My father would have cheerfully offered me as collateral in a game of checkers. And likely did." He'd shaken his head. "What could possibly be worse than the things he already felt comfortable foisting upon the entire world?"

"I thought you might ask that," the other man had said, with entirely too much satisfaction in his voice.

That had been Orion's first inkling that this was all worse than he'd thought.

Aristotle pulled out a file and placed it on the table between them. A low coffee table where he could, with what seemed to Orion to be great relish, flip through the photographs he'd brought with him.

It took three pictures.

Orion sat back, feeling faintly sick.

And with those images in his head that he knew he would never be able to wash clean.

The man across from him hadn't laughed, though there was a look about him that suggested he would, later.

"Tempting, isn't it, to imagine that with the old man dead and buried, all his scandalous acts are swept away. But I think you see, now, that there are some things that can never go away. And more important, that you too will find yourself tainted if they are exposed." Aristotle had smiled again. "Your Majesty."

For a moment, Orion hadn't been sure that he could speak. And he had been closer to indulging the tidal wave of fury inside him than he ever had been before.

It took everything he had not to launch himself at the other man. Everything he had and the sure knowledge that Aristotle would love it if he did.

But everything in him had rebelled. Giving in to blackmail was never the right answer. He knew that. It had been impressed upon him from a young age that he must never allow another person to have that kind of hold

over him, not when he would one day rule—
except, what choice did he have?

Idylla could not stand another scandal.

And certainly not one that was, though it
beggared belief, worse than all that had come
before.

Aristotle had waited, the very picture of
corpulent malice.

And, as ever, Orion had shoved his personal
feelings aside and thought of the kingdom.

"I do not know what bargain you made with
my father," he had said eventually, though
every word was like poison on his tongue.
"Therefore, I cannot honor it. If you want
your daughter to be my queen, you must
agree to my terms."

Aristotle had chuckled. "That's not how
this works."

But the longer Orion gazed at him, expres-
sionless, the less he laughed.

And when he stopped, Orion continued.
"You will sign a binding legal document that
will ensure two things. One, that you will
be imprisoned for life if you violate any of
the terms in said document, all of which, of
course, will insist upon your silence regard-

ing these photos. And two, in addition to your jail time, you will be fined. To the point of insolvency and beyond, if you are ever responsible for any of this coming to light. Do you understand me?"

Aristotle sputtered. "I don't think—"

But Orion had spent his whole life dealing with a man just like Aristotle. A man who was even worse, in fact, because his every word had been law, like it or not. Once the red edge of his temper had faded, he'd understood that like it or not, he was in his element.

He would be handling his father unto eternity, it seemed.

But at least he was good at that.

"In return," he said coldly, "I will elevate your vile, polluted bloodline. I will marry your daughter. I will do this because unlike my father, I am a man of my word." He'd watched Aristotle's face grow mottled. "But because I am my father's son, I will also put the betrothal agreement in writing." He'd taken out his mobile and fired off a series of texts to his staff. "I will have my attorneys deliver the appropriate documents while we wait for the search on your properties to be finished."

And Aristotle hadn't liked it but he'd nodded, anyway, and made the deal.

There were worse things, Orion told himself now as he opened the French doors and stepped out onto the balcony. Men in his position had been marrying for reasons like this, or worse, as long as there had been kings. So it went. His own parents' marriage had been arranged and if he knew nothing else it was that without even trying, he would be a better husband than his father had been.

No matter if Calista Skyros was a carbon copy of her repellant father.

He was sure that the woman who stood at the balcony rail, her gaze somewhere in the distance where the Aegean met the sky, heard his approach. But she didn't turn.

And whether she had a sense of the dramatic, was deliberately being rude, or was girding her loins for this confrontation, he didn't know. But he took the opportunity to do the same.

Orion had seen pictures of her, of course. His staff had presented him with an exhaustive portfolio on Lady Calista within hours of his father's initial announcement. He knew she'd been educated at the Sorbonne, not at an Idyllian university. That she had been bred to make an aristocratic marriage, regardless of her father's filthy trade, because that was how Idyllian nobility worked. Its purpose was to continue itself.

He knew that after the Sorbonne, Calista had come back to Idylla and started work at the lowest level of her father's company, which he was sure was meant to counteract suggestions of nepotism when it was clearly the opposite. These days, she had clawed her way much higher in the company. She was now the vice president of a media conglomerate that trafficked in lies.

His betrothed was a liar by blood and by choice, in other words.

She was in no way an appropriate choice to be his queen. If he'd been permitted to choose for himself, he would have looked for someone who worked with charities. Someone whose calling in life was service to others, not…revolting tabloid speculation.

But Orion was a practical, rational man.

He'd had to be, whether he wanted to be or not. The truth was, he had never expected that he might get the opportunity to fall in love like a regular person. Because he wasn't one.

In a way, this was no different from any arrangement that might have been made for him.

And all that mattered was that he would protect Idylla, come what may. Even if it meant marrying this creature and linking her detestable family to his.

He had placed the Crown of Idylla upon his head and he had sworn to do his duty, and so he would.

She turned then, and for a moment, Orion didn't think of duty at all.

His betrothed was not the least bit photogenic, he understood in a searing, unexpected flash of what he was appalled to understand was desire.

Electric and near overwhelming.

Every photograph he'd seen of his intended had led him to expect that she would be pretty. In that way that so many slender blonde women were pretty. Not quite interchangeable, but then again, the world was filled with them. One blended into the next.

But Calista Skyros was not the blandly pretty blonde she'd appeared in photographs.

There was something about her. Something about the way she held herself, maybe. Or the surprising, sparkling intelligence in her aquamarine gaze. She was blonde, yes. And pretty, inarguably.

But something in him pulled tight and seemed to *hum* as he gazed at her, and he had not been prepared for that.

For what seemed like an eternity, their eyes caught and held, out there on the windswept balcony.

And Orion was uncomfortably aware of himself as a man, not a king. Flesh and blood and need, to his horror.

"Your Majesty," she said in quiet greeting, and he was sure some kind of shadow moved over her face.

It only made her prettier. And more interesting. She straightened from the rail as she faced him, then sank before him in the expected deep curtsy, exhibiting both an easy grace and the kind of excellent manners that would have told him of her years of comportment classes if he hadn't already known.

He would have said such displays were fussy, old-fashioned window dressing he could do without, but the sight of Calista Skyros genuflecting before him made everything inside him tighten, then shift.

She rose with the same ease and he studied her, this woman who would be his queen. His wife. The mother of his heirs.

It seemed an odd thing indeed to stand on this familiar balcony while cool November air came in off the ocean, with an edge to it despite the sun, and think so dispassionately about *his wife*. About the sex he would have with this stranger to ensure his line of succession. About the relationship they would be forced to cobble together because of those things, one way or another. Toward the end of his mother's life his parents had been separated by as many layers of staff and physical distance inside this palace as possible, but Orion had always hoped he could create some kind of harmony in something so cold-blooded.

And yet what he thought when he looked at her was…not harmonious.

Not precisely.

He forced himself to remember who she was.

"Lady Calista," he said coolly by way of greeting, inclining his head.

He could not fault her appearance in any way, though he wanted to find nothing but faults in her. That would be easier, some-how, but unlike her father, she was flawless. She wore a long-sleeved dress in a soft dove-gray color that flattered her features and was both modest and modern at once. She wore pearls at her ears, and though the brisk sea air rushed around them, her hair stayed put in its sleek chignon.

He felt his jaw tighten, because, of course, she was auditioning for the role of queen. A role she knew she'd already won, perhaps. But that being the case, she could have rolled into this meeting like a publicity disaster waiting to happen—simply to show him how little control he had, as he suspected her father would have if he was her—and she hadn't.

Orion would take his triumphs where he could.

"Perhaps we can step inside," he said, because maybe it was the sea air and the view that was getting to him. Maybe the usual Idyllian sun was making her appear lovelier and less patently evil than she was. Inside the palace, surely, reality would reassert itself. "We have much to discuss."

She smiled in a quick sort of way that made him imagine she felt awkward, though that was unlikely.

Beware the urge to consider her a pawn in this, he growled at himself. *She is the vice president of her father's company, not a sacrificial virgin he's offered up in tribute.*

Whatever she was, he ushered her indoors with exaggerated courtesy, then sat across from her on a set of antique sofas that dated from the fifteenth century.

And then instantly regretted it.

Because it was quieter in here. More intimate, and the last thing in the world he wanted was intimacy with a member of the Skyros family.

If his parents' twisted relationship had been

any indication, intimacy was not a prerequisite for the royal marriage. Or even particularly desirable, for that matter.

He didn't know how long he sat there, studying her as if the force of his attention could render her as bland as he'd expected her to be. But when he realized they were sitting in silence, and would continue to do so because he was the king and should speak first, he cleared his throat.

"Thank you for coming today," he said, sounding stiff and formal and pompous, which struck him as far more appropriate than standing about on balconies, confusing himself. "I thought it was best for the two of us to meet before our official engagement announcement."

He paused, and she seemed to startle, as if she'd never heard of such a thing. "Of course. Yes. The official announcement."

That struck him as disingenuous, but he wrestled his temper into place, locked up tight inside him.

"It will take place in two days' time, at the first holiday ball of the season." She didn't react to that, so he carried on with his talking points. "We will discuss our whirlwind relationship and how it was a bright light during the dark days before and after my father's death. We will talk about hope, and a new dawn, not only for ourselves, but for Idylla. As is tradition, we will be married six weeks from the first ball, on Christmas Eve, captivating the hearts and minds of not only the kingdom, but the world. Yet as spectacular as our wedding will be, as is customary, our marriage will be reserved. Competent."

"And sane," she chimed in. And smiled when he lifted a brow at her, though he rather thought the curve of her lips had an edge to it. That was unexpected. "Forgive me, Your Majesty. But I have heard your speeches."

Was that a slap at him? He shoved it aside. "Excellent. Then you already know how things will go."

"I admire your..." She paused. *"...certainty."*

"I am certain," Orion said quietly. "Because I will make it so."

"How...monocratic."

"Indeed. As I am the monarch." He waited for her to swallow, hard. "I will marry you, Lady Calista, because I gave my word that I

would. I will make you my queen and consort, because that is the bargain your father
made with mine. But hear me."

And this time, she only stared back at him
mutely. No clever comments at the ready.

"I will tolerate no scandals," he told her.
"And I understand that this might be hard
for you, as scandals are your stock in trade."
He saw something flash in her eyes like the
sea, but she only pressed her lips into a firm
line. "But there will be no anonymous stories
from this palace. There will be no salacious
insider exposés. If you cannot comply with
this requirement, I am sorry to tell you that
you will find our marriage…challenging."

"'Challenging?'" Her voice was huskier
than before. "What, precisely, does 'challenging' mean?"

He allowed himself a faint smile. "I will
take a page from kings of old," he told her,
the vow of it in his voice. He felt certain she
could hear it. "If you defy me I will install
you in Castle Crag."

"Castle Crag." She blinked. "You don't
mean *Castle Crag*."

"I have never meant anything more."

"Castle Crag is in the middle of the Aegean." She stared at him, her eyes widening at whatever she saw. "It's a slab of rock with an ancient fortress on it. I don't think it has electricity. It's a *prison*."

"That is precisely why any number of my ancestors preferred to keep their wives and assorted other dissidents there," Orion said, his voice even and his gaze hard on hers. "I plan to rule as a progressive king, Lady Calista. But when it comes to the queen I was blackmailed into accepting, know this. Where you are concerned, you can expect me to be purely medieval."

CHAPTER TWO

CALISTA SKYROS COULD have gone her whole life without ever meeting the King of Idylla.

That would have been her preference, in fact, because she liked the royal family well enough—but only in a distant sense. As pomp, circumstance, and background noise to the real work that went on in the island kingdom.

But since when had her father ever taken her preferences into account?

She stared at the man before her. Because he was a man, she reminded herself. A man who happened to be a king, sure. But no matter how her mother fluttered around her— insisting that she dress like Idylla's answer to one of those overexposed British princesses—or her father growled at her about his *agenda*, Calista's goals did not involve palace intrigue. Or calling herself queen of anything, for that matter, no matter how many fancy dresses might be involved.

Her goals had always been simple.

Protect her sister. Neutralize her parents. And while she was at it, take over Skyros Media, oust her father from the board, and control her own destiny, at last.

It was all very simple indeed, if not as easy as she'd hoped when she'd started down this path years ago. Regardless, she was so close now. So close she could taste it. She had every reason to believe Skyros Media would be hers by the end of the year.

At last.

Her father had come to her when the news of evil old King Max's death had reached him, puffed up with malicious joy that he would be installing his eldest daughter in the palace at last.

Not that Aristotle Skyros called her his *eldest* daughter. He liked to refer to her as his *only* daughter, which made Melody laugh but was one more reason Calista loathed him.

For a moment, she'd forgotten to pretend that she wanted the things he did, her usual gambit when dealing with him. For a moment, she'd forgotten that she wasn't out of the woods just yet.

"Not this betrothal nonsense again," she'd said, blinking at him over a mountain of paperwork on her desk in Skyros Media headquarters, there in the center of the royal city that spread out in a crescent below the palace and reminded her daily that she could endure as it had. "You can't be serious."

That had been a mistake. She hadn't been thinking, too focused on how close she was to the end result she'd been pushing for all this time. Her entire life, it seemed—but she hadn't made it there yet.

"Don't you dare take that tone with me," her father had snarled, that dangerous note in his voice. The one Calista had gone out of her way to avoid hearing for years now—and had been mostly successful. Because she'd convinced him that she was obedient. His protégé, desperate for his approval. His successor who followed his every command. As close as it was possible to get to the son he'd always wanted but had never had.

But she knew in that moment that if she'd

been within reach, he would have slapped her soundly.

Don't go and ruin everything now, she'd warned herself.

"I'm sorry," she'd said at once, the conciliatory tone bitter on her tongue. She'd tried to shift her body language where she sat, hunching her shoulders and making herself small, the way she'd used to do. Back when she'd been a girl, and her father's rages had been a daily, inescapable trial there'd been no hope of escaping. "I just… Me as a queen? I can't imagine it, Papa."

She hated that word. *Papa.* As if there was some affection between them. As if her father was capable of such a thing as a paternal feeling. Or feelings at all.

But long ago, she'd learned how to soothe him, and calling him *papa* as if she admired and revered him was one method. Sometimes the only way to make it through life in her father's fist was to bow and scrape a little and tell him only things he wished to hear. As she'd grown, she'd learned that what a man like her father truly wanted from her was accomplishments he could claim as his own.

So she'd thrown herself headfirst into making them happen.

She hadn't gotten herself in a situation where she needed to be *quite so* conciliatory in a long while. She couldn't say she liked the feeling.

Calista had been relieved to discover that she still had the knack for calming him when he settled himself in the chair on the other side of her desk, looking less furious and more…avid. She'd had to fight to conceal her shudder of distaste.

"I paid a great deal of money to secure your betrothal to Max's royal spawn," he'd told her, the remnants of his infamous temper still a little too obvious in his voice. "I expect you to honor that investment with a formal engagement and wedding."

"Of course, Papa," she'd murmured, aiming for *sweet* and *humble*. "Have I ever let you down?"

Calista was able to make herself say such things because she knew full well that the takeover she'd been planning for years was close. The annual board meeting was December 23. That gave her what was left of the year to make sure all her ducks were in a row. Everything she wanted was *so close* within her grasp she could almost reach out and touch it with her fingertips—

But if she got ahead of herself, she'd ruin everything. Overconfidence would lead straight to a loss. She knew that. Just as she knew she needed to win.

So despite her feelings on the subject, Calista had agreed to go ahead with this ridiculous engagement. And the wedding, she understood, theoretically would follow it. She had no other choice. Or, more accurately, her father had assumed she was fully on board because she knew better than to argue with him. It was pointless. Aristotle was obsessed with marrying her off to the brand-new king, and fighting with him about it would only get in the way of her true aims.

But she certainly hadn't expected it to take so long to get her first audience with King Orion. His father had died in the summer and here it was November. She'd had to spend months acting as if she was not only interested in marrying the man, but devastated that he was ignoring their betrothal. She'd had to listen to her father complain endlessly about the situation and about how it was a personal insult to him.

Worse, she'd had to suffer her sister's unapologetic cackling about her upcoming *royal wedding*.

Still, Calista had come here today prepared to do what she needed to do. Pretend anything, act any part to hasten this along—not because she wanted to marry anyone, much less the king, but because it would give her father something to focus on while she gutted his company and made it her own. And the more her father focused on himself, the less he was likely to turn his attention to Melody.

Calista was determined to keep him from concentrating on her younger sister, no matter what.

But as she stared back at the new, young king, having acquitted herself marvelously— if she said so herself—with a little of those noble manners her teachers in boarding school had claimed she would never learn, she found herself revising her thinking on this whole big mess.

Because if what her father had ranted repeatedly was true, King Orion *had* to marry her.

He didn't have a choice in the matter.

And that meant Calista didn't have to fall all over him. She didn't have to pander to him, or try to smooth things over with him the way she did with her father. Unless she was very much mistaken, it meant she had to do nothing at all but show up.

"I'm not interested in any scandals either, actually," she said now, with images of remote Castle Crag still spinning around in her head. She folded her hands in her lap, presenting him with the perfect posture she liked to roll out in the boardroom, where no one expected much from the blonde, pretty daughter of such a hateful man. They looked at her and saw a bimbo. Which was usually right about when she whipped around and sank her teeth into their jugulars. "But I'm also not interested in being threatened with fortresses on rocks a million miles from shore."

He…froze. "I beg your pardon?"

Slipping back into her familiar corporate mode was comforting. Because there was something about King Orion that made Calista…edgy. He wasn't what she'd expected, maybe. For one thing, the approximately seven trillion photographs she'd seen of him in her lifetime didn't really capture him. He looked like the images she'd seen, with his close-cropped chestnut hair, grave hazel eyes, and that stern mouth. It was just that, put all together, he was a lot more than a novelty tea towel sold to tourists in all the shops.

A *lot* more.

Her chest felt a bit tight and her pulse was a bit dramatic, if she was honest.

Part of it was that he was so shockingly fit. Rangy muscle, surprisingly solid, and packaged into a dark suit that should have made him look stuffy. But instead, it was cut so well that she found herself feeling remarkably patriotic about the way the fabric clung to his wide shoulders.

Even as he sat there and made pronouncements about what she would or wouldn't do, all she *wanted* to do was move a little closer to see whether or not his abdomen was as hard and ridged as she suspected it was.

But more than all of that, it was that air around him. As if he emitted his own electrical charge. There was a sense of leashed power in him, in the way he held himself and *waited*, almost, that she had not been expecting.

The same way she hadn't been expecting a hollow, hungry thing deep in her belly to hum at the sight of him.

You need to get your act together, Calista, she snapped at herself. Because she had far too much riding on all of this to lose her head over a handsome man.

Even if the handsome man in question was her king.

And, more, thought she was going to marry him and produce babies on command.

"It seems to me that you're under the impression that you have control here." She smiled, that little curve of her lips that business associates liked to claim was enigmatic. Usually after she'd pummeled them into dust. "But my understanding is that you actually *have to* marry me. Whether you want to or not."

He stared at her, that same frozen and arrested expression on his face. "Am I to understand that you know about the—ah—*leverage* your father has used against me?"

Aristotle had ranted excessively about the fact he had something on the old king that the new king would kill to conceal. He had not shared what that leverage was.

Something Calista saw no reason to share with the man staring her down.

"The point is that the leverage exists," she said, because she had always been good at playing these little power games. "And it exists on you, not me. So I'll thank you to stop making threats about Castle Crag. I have no interest in playing Knights of the Crusades, or whatever your threats of going medieval are supposed to mean. As far as I'm concerned, this is a business proposition between our two families, nothing more. Which is medieval enough, I'd think."

She thought she'd startled him. Or maybe she only wanted to. An expression she couldn't name and certainly couldn't read flashed through his eyes, then disappeared into a flash of grave hazel.

"How refreshing," he said after a long moment, though she doubted very much he found her the least bit refreshing. "I was led to expect the usual princess fantasies."

Calista laughed. "I can't think of anything I would like to be less than a princess. Luckily, what we're talking about is my becoming a queen, not a princess. I can get my head around that."

"Am I to understand you see yourself as one already? Metaphorically speaking, of course."

"I'm a businesswoman, not a queen," she replied, her heart beating a little faster because he'd challenged her, however obliquely. "And let me set the mood here, to save us some time. I don't care what your relationship is with my father."

"I would never describe the interactions I have been forced to have with your father as a 'relationship.'"

King Orion's voice was so frigid she was faintly surprised icicles didn't sprout into being round the room. Suddenly, it felt like November in a more northern, snow-covered place, instead of the typically mild Novembers here in Idylla's balmy Mediterranean climate.

She told herself she was immune to the cold. "Whatever you want to call it, I'm not interested in it. I'm sure you have your reasons for bowing to my father's whims and accepting this ridiculous betrothal. But whatever those reasons might be, it means only that you, like so many others, have surrendered to his blackmail."

"Again, I would dispute those terms."

She waved a hand. "Dispute them all you like. It doesn't change the facts. You're in his pocket, which means you're now in mine. And who knows? I've never had my own king before. Maybe it will be fun."

And she watched, fascinated despite herself, as King Orion Augustus Pax looked at her as if his head was exploding. Internally, of course.

Externally, all she could see was a muscle flexing in his lean jaw. And that fire that turned his hazel gaze to gold.

Despite herself, her breath caught. She suddenly wondered what it would be like if the most controlled creature in the history of the world—something that had been apparent when King Orion was no more than a princeling, especially when stood next to his disaster of a father—let go.

Could he let go?

She felt goose bumps shiver down the length of her spine.

Orion's eyes were volcanic. But his voice was calm. "I will remind you, Lady Calista, that I am your king."

"I do know that, Your Majesty. That's why I curtsied."

She made her voice careless, but the seething heat that was blasting her way was more uncomfortable than she wanted to admit. She got to her feet as if this was her meeting. Her darling little room tucked away in the royal palace, and the man before her nothing but… some guy.

Though no one could possibly confuse King Orion for *some guy*.

Just as, no matter what she'd said, it was hard to imagine a man so electric and indisputably regal in anyone's pocket, either. Even if she knew that he was. Her father had made certain to brag excessively that he was the architect of this betrothal, as if she wouldn't have figured that out on her own.

"This must be hard for you," she said, moving to look at the pictures scattered on the dreadfully elegant sideboard. Pictures of the two princes. The former queen. And not a one of King Max, which she supposed was only to be expected. She had yet to meet a soul who missed him, except possibly her father. And not because he'd had any affection for the dissipated late king. But because he'd been so easy to manipulate.

"Which part?" Orion's question was crisp. A bit like a slap. "The part where, for my father's sins, I am forced to contend with a base, repulsive reptile like Aristotle Skyros? Or the part where, having accepted that I must do my duty to my country even in the face of such an insult, I am confronted with a craven display of overweening self-importance that I must crown and call my queen?"

Ouch.

But she laughed and she couldn't have said why. "*Overweening* is quite a word, Your Majesty. Though I think you'll find that what men consider self-importance in women is usually the sort of confidence they consider par for the course in a man."

"On the contrary, Lady Calista." And that light in his hard gaze made her want to shiver. "Were any man to dare speak to me as you have just now I would lay him out flat."

Her curse was that some part of her longed to see it.

She made a tsking sound, and found herself leaning back against the sideboard in what was, she could admit, a bit of a show. How could she help herself? She was being forced into an arranged marriage against her will. That was the long and the short of it, and no matter her intentions where that was concerned or her reasons for going along with it, a girl had to make her own fun.

And you're in no way trying to cover up your response to the man, a voice inside her that sounded a lot like her sister's chimed in.

"Violence is something we expect from your brother, King Orion," she said, ignoring that voice. "Never you. Never the desperately responsible crown prince and possible savior of our dissipated country, a man so excruciatingly polite and correct that no one has ever been able to dig up the names of his lovers."

The king did not rise. He did not lounge back in his seat. He did not fidget, adjust his clothing, or shift his weight—and yet she still had the impression that he gathered himself. And changed, somehow, the very composition of his body. Right there before her eyes.

She told herself she was being foolish. But all the while, that gaze of his grew ever more molten.

"I imagine that must be a favorite pursuit in a media enterprise of such journalistic integrity as Skyros Media." His voice was a sardonic lash and it cost Calista something not to wince. "Rifling about in the trash for private information that is none of your concern."

She lifted her chin. "I think the word you're looking for is *news*."

"There is nothing newsworthy in someone's personal life. It is private and personal, by definition."

"I was under the impression that you were the king of this country," she shot back, lifting her brows at him. "Can a king have a personal life? I rather thought that what you do with the life your subjects support is our business. Either way, the choices you make personally affect us all. Or did you miss out on the entirety of your father's reign?"

Something blazed in his gaze then, and she expected him to erupt. To shoot to his feet. To hit something.

Or even raise his voice.

But instead, King Orion stayed where he was.

Locked down, she found herself thinking. Frozen solid.

And she didn't know why she had the sudden, sharp urge to see if she could melt him, by any means necessary.

When he spoke, she couldn't repress a shiver, because his voice was perfectly even. Measured. As if there had been nothing the least bit volcanic here when she was sure she could still taste the ash in the elegant room all around them.

"If your aim was to impress upon me that you will do as you like, consider it done." He studied her, and to her surprise, she almost felt as if she might...blush. Something she didn't think she'd done in her entire life—not when she'd grown up under Aristotle's thumb. Thankfully, the odd, prickling feeling passed. "I appreciate you coming into this meeting prepared to show me exactly who you are, Lady Calista. I assure you I won't forget it."

That, too, was a threat. And a more effective one, perhaps, because he said it so calmly.

"If you think I'm going to curl up in a ball and cry because you don't approve of me, think again," she told him, striving for the same tone, and refusing to duck her head or make herself smaller. There was only one man she pretended to cower before, and it wasn't this one. No matter if, deep inside, there was that *humming*. "I've agreed to marry you, Your Majesty. I'm fully aware of what that means."

"Are you?" He tilted his head slightly to one side. "I wonder. For example, can I expect this same aggression in bed?"

Again, a prickling heat swept over her, and horrified her. Worse, there was a gleam in the midst of all that stern hazel that told her he knew it. He *knew* he affected her.

When Calista had spent all these years learning how to conceal her feelings so well she sometimes wondered if she had any left.

She met his gaze as if he didn't trouble her in the least. "If you had the slightest idea how to be aggressive in bed or anywhere else, Your Majesty, I feel certain we would have found evidence of that by now." Calista allowed herself a smirk. "And run it in our tabloids, of course."

To her surprise, he laughed. "Is that how you measure things, then? Whether or not it shows up in one of your sick, sad little magazines?"

"I believe in a free press. Was that the question?"

Orion looked entirely too satisfied, and she hated that something deep in her belly *quivered*. "I'll take that to mean you haven't the slightest idea what you're getting into with me, Lady Calista. How delightful to find we have something in common."

She felt breathless again, and had to remind herself that no matter what happened here in the battle for control over their dreary arranged marriage, it didn't change reality. And the reality was that he could talk a big game, but he had no power here. He could go on all he liked about his reserved, competent, sane rule, but he had no control over her or what she did or if she was any of those things.

She would go along with this betrothal because it served her ends, not his. And because it did, she would go to these balls, announce their engagement in front of the whole world, and if necessary, even marry him on Christmas Eve in accordance with tradition. Who cared?

Because as soon as she made her move and took over her father's company, it didn't matter whether she was a queen or not. She would be the owner of Skyros Media and she would finally be in the power position over her father, and able to make sure that no matter what happened, Melody would be safe.

She'd worked her whole life to get to this place.

What did she care where King Orion was in all of that?

"Since we're speaking so frankly," he said, and she got the strangest sensation, then. It was almost as if he could read her every last thought. But that was impossible. He was a stranger and she'd been told a thousand times that she was unreadable. "I should tell you that I will insist on fidelity."

"Of course you will." She rolled her eyes and got the distinct impression that no one else had dared do such a thing in his exalted presence. So she did it again. "That must be one of those king things."

"It's one of those funny little *king things*, yes. The royal bloodline determines the line of succession and the throne of Idylla, which has been in my family for centuries." His stern mouth almost curved. Calista almost shivered. "You will find, I think, that most people in my position feel strongly about such things."

"Let me tell you how I see my role as queen," Calista replied, in a brighter tone than strictly necessary. "I can dress the part. But if you expect me to look adoring or fold my hands awkwardly while standing obediently behind you, that's not going to work."

"You are of noble blood, Lady Calista. Surely you are aware that there are certain rules of etiquette. One of them, I am very much afraid, is that you cannot precede your king."

She sighed. "I understand etiquette, thank you. But you need to know, right now, that I have no intention of pretending I'm subservient to any man. King or otherwise."

"Of course not." His voice was soothing. Too soothing, she realized. "That is why you have agreed to marry a total stranger. Because you are in no way subject to your father's demands."

"For all you know I agitated for this job."

She should not have said that. It had been a reaction, not strategic at all, and she regretted it at once. And then regretted it even more when those eyes of his glowed gold, and she knew beyond a shadow of a doubt that he was somehow aware he'd scored points.

"I am delighted that you understand that it is, in fact, a job." He nodded toward the windows, somehow incorporating the whole of the island with a single peremptory gesture. "Idylla is an ancient kingdom. Small but independent. An independence that historically came with a price."

"Are you…telling me the history of my own country?"

"The history of this country is the history of my family, Lady Calista. Yours, I believe, was elevated to nobility a great many centuries after the first in my line took the throne."

"Oh, I see," she said after a moment. After that sunk in. "You don't have the power in this interaction that you think you should, so you need to turn it into a measure of your manhood. In this case, a *purer blood than thou* contest. Too bad blood isn't actually blue. Or we could each open up a vein and see whose better matches the sky."

"You missed my meaning entirely," Orion said calmly. She decided she hated that tone he took. Its very calmness was offensive. "The fact is, with a few notable exceptions like my own father, my line has held the throne throughout the ages because members of my family have always been aware that a king can only be as effective as he is loved."

"Loved by whom?" she asked, with a laugh.

And she ignored the fact that the laugh felt a great deal more brittle than it should have.

"I do not require your love, never fear,"

Orion said coolly. And, once again, he made her imagine for a terrible moment that she might actually flush beet red. Like some silly girl, when she was anything but. "I require you to do your job. And no, that does not involve making cow's eyes at me before the cameras, though I would prefer it if you did not scowl. That is not good optics, as I believe someone in your profession should know. But all of that is window dressing."

"Window dressing? I would have assumed you had staff for such things."

"Your actual job is really very simple, Lady Calista," he told her in the same cool, intense way. "All you need to do is provide me with an heir."

Something fairly sizzled between them at that. Much as Calista wanted to deny it.

She felt her breath punch out of her lungs. She felt her body change, growing hot and heavy.

Though she would die before she let him know that he had that effect on her.

She would die before she admitted that the idea of making heirs with him suddenly seemed a lot more interesting to her than

wresting control of her father's company—
because it was a betrayal of everything she'd
worked for.

It was a betrayal of her sister, herself, and
the things they'd held dear their whole lives.

It was a betrayal, plain and simple, and she
loathed herself for even a moment's lapse
from her primary goal, even if only in her
own head.

She made herself laugh instead. As insult-
ingly as possible.

"You don't have to dress it up, Your Majesty," she drawled, and smirked at him. Edgy
and tight. "You could have just said you want
to have sex with me. You don't have to pretend it's for the greater good."

CHAPTER THREE

TWO DAYS LATER, like it or not, Orion found himself getting ready for the first of the traditional Idylla Christmas balls he would share with his betrothed—soon to be his fiancée.

And if he wasn't mistaken, he was actually...filled with a kind of anticipation.

Though he told himself it was not as simple as that.

He'd assumed that their initial meeting would sort things out between them and make their respective roles clear. He'd expected Lady Calista would be like any of the typical Idyllian nobility he'd contended with in his time. She'd been meant to fawn all over him and tremble and agree with his every utterance, pretending she was a vestal virgin instead of the usual party girl. His staff had assured him that while, yes, she had a place in her father's company, it was only for show.

But she hadn't done any of the things he'd expected she would.

To say that their first meeting had not gone according to plan was vastly understating things.

She'd underscored that by continuing to do nothing but laugh, at him, clearly and boldly—and then leaving. Without waiting to be dismissed from his presence.

And more to the point, without agreeing to a single one of his terms. Or even pretending to consider them.

He had no idea what to expect from her now.

Orion had spent entirely too much time since then trying to reconcile who he'd imagined she was based on the depth of her curtsy and the demure outfit she'd worn with who she'd proved herself to be thereafter.

He was appalled at himself, actually.

If he thought about it, he should have assumed that a man like Aristotle Skyros could, naturally, bring into the world only creatures of selfish greed and astonishingly bad behavior just like himself. There was nothing surprising about it.

What Orion couldn't countenance was his reaction to her.

Everything she'd said and done had horrified him on every level, obviously. But his body had taken a different tack despite that. His body—which he had long treated with a monastic fervor Griffin liked to tell him took zealotry to a new level—did not seem to care that Lady Calista was nothing at all like the queen he'd imagined would rule at his side. His body had not been overly concerned with her disrespect, her flippant responses, her outright rudeness to both her king and her future husband.

His body had gone rogue.

Orion had woken in the night, hard and aching. And no amount of exercise, cold showers, or sheer fury at his own flesh had helped. The only thing that had was a detailed fantasy about what it would be like to feel that sharp tongue of hers on that place where he was hardest of all.

Damn her.

Orion prided himself on being in control. Of himself, his body and his mind, in every regard. It was another decision he had made a long, long time ago, faced with the knowledge that one of the great many ways his father was weak was King Max's inability to deny his appetites. Particularly those of the flesh.

Orion had decided that he would be master of his own body in the same way that he had learned to master his emotions. He stayed in control, always, no matter the provocation.

Calista Skyros tested him. She tested his control.

And he hated it.

But he hadn't lost a test yet.

Grimly, Orion allowed his fussy, demanding valet to finish dressing him in the exquisite black-tie ensemble appropriate for the occasion of the first ball of the Idyllian holiday season. The ball that happened to also be the place where the newly crowned king would announce his engagement, God help him. Once he was suitably regal, he walked through the palace to meet the woman he would never have chosen to be his bride, especially now that he'd met her. There in the same private salon where he'd faced the unpleasant fact that he was not as immune to a blackmailer's daughter as he should have been.

Perhaps the truth was that he was still trying to face that fact.

This time, when he opened the door and stepped inside, the room was not empty.

It was, in fact, rather more full than he had been anticipating. He was displeased to note that Calista had come with her father and mother in tow. Something he was sure he ought to have been horrified by.

But for the moment, a very long moment that seemed to drag out for an eternity, all he could see was her.

Just her, as if there was a separate sun that was all hers and it shined on only her, even at night.

He dismissed the strange, almost poetic notion and focused on this woman he was bound to marry, but that was no better. Because she was even prettier than the last time he'd seen her, which should not have been possible. And even though he knew now that the *something* about her he'd been unable to name on the balcony two days ago was the same sort of malice her father wore visibly on his skin, his body didn't know the difference. Tonight she wore a dramatic gown, a dress that sparkled and made her look exactly like a girl with a princess fantasy only he could make come true, when he now knew she was nothing of the kind.

Did he want that kind of woman? Wrapped up in some kind of a fairy tale when the reality of royal life was far less shiny and sweet? Before meeting Calista, Orion would have sworn he did not. But that was before she had haunted him, simply by looking at him as if *she* was in control of things.

She smirked at him again now, which he already both detested and found sent a heat spiraling deep into him.

Making him ache anew.

"I take it that when you're a king, you don't have to observe typical first-date protocols. Like picking a girl up at her own house, rather than forcing her to traipse all the way to the palace to act overawed and under-royal."

That was her greeting to her future husband, lord and king.

Orion could not have said why it was he wanted to smile.

"Kings do not go on first dates, Lady Calista," he said. Forbiddingly. "Nor do they dance attendance at the front doors of their lessers. The nation would revolt at the very idea."

And he enjoyed that too much, maybe. Because judging by their reactions, neither Skyros nor his daughter considered themselves *less than* anything—and particularly not less than their king.

But it was Skyros's wife who surprised Orion the most. She was the one who'd dropped into a spine-crackingly low curtsy at the sight of him. She rose now, long after she'd descended, her carriage painfully erect. And she glared at her husband and daughter in turn.

"We do not treat the King of Idylla with disrespect," she hissed. "*We* know our duty."

"Spare me the royalist rantings, Appollonia," Aristotle growled. But even so, he performed a perfunctory bow, almost as if he worried someone might be hid behind the paintings, recording the meeting. Then, to Orion's astonishment, Calista curtsied, too.

But when she rose, she fixed Orion with her own fierce glare. As if she was daring him to comment on the fact that her mother still held sway over her behavior. At least in public.

He tucked that away like a small, handy knife in his boot—the kind Griffin carried about with him ever since his time in the military.

"I hope you're both prepared for this tonight," Aristotle said then, puffing himself up with his usual self-importance, his beady eyes all over Orion as if he was not a king, but a piece of meat for the carving. "Everybody loves a royal love story and the two of you need to sell it."

Orion did not dignify that with a response. Particularly when the response he had in mind involved the Royal Guard.

"Papa." To his surprise, the smirk on Calista's lips changed to a far more engaging smile when she aimed it at her father, though Orion found he believed it less. "This isn't a love story. You know that."

"It doesn't matter what it *is*," Aristotle retorted, with a laugh that made him seem even oilier than before. "No one cares about what's real, Calista. What matters is what I can sell."

And he kept his gaze fixed on Orion on the off chance he was confused as to who was the greater commodity here.

Odious, appalling man.

Soon to be your father-in-law, a dark voice in him intoned.

It was unbearable.

"Thank you," Orion said. With all the authority in him. "I would now like a few moments alone with Lady Calista, please."

And he inclined his head in a manner that made it clear he was not making a request.

Aristotle grumbled, but his wife managed to somehow genuflect while removing herself from the room, backward. A feat that would have impressed Orion, but then the door closed behind Aristotle and Appollonia Skyros.

Leaving just the two of them in the room. Orion and Calista.

He should not have let that simple fact work its way beneath his skin, all heat and need.

The way she did, too, doing nothing more than standing there looking like a proper royal princess, save for the smirk on her clever mouth and the challenge in her aquamarine gaze.

He reminded himself that he was meant to be deeply appalled, but she was wearing a sweeping, romantic gown and he wanted to put his hands on her more than he should have wanted anything that in no way benefited his kingdom, and he couldn't quite make himself believe that he was *appalled* at all.

"Do you have more demands for me to refuse?" Calista asked. And Orion really should have found himself sickened by the tone she used. So disrespectful. So patently challenging. So invigorating, if he was honest, after a day crammed full of deadly dull policy advisers and pompous cabinet ministers. "That sounds like fun to me."

"Not quite," he said.

He reached into his pocket and withdrew the small, velvet pouch he'd slipped in there earlier, despite his valet's protestations that it *murdered the line* of his suit. He pretended he did not notice the way she watched him, or the way she stood there before him, stiffly, as if she didn't know how to anticipate what he might do next.

Orion sensed he had the advantage, and he knew he should seize it, utilize it—

But first he had to do this. It was tradition, no matter the circumstances of their betrothal, and he was nothing if not a slave to tradition.

He upended the pouch and shook out the ring inside it. And he knew he didn't imagine the quick indrawn breath he heard from Calista when it landed on his palm.

"This is the foremost crown jewel of Idylla," he told her, though he expected she already knew it. He held the ring there where it had landed, gleaming in the lamplight and seeming to take on a life of its own—as if all the legends that had ever been told about it were there in its stones and shimmer. "It is always worn by the Queen of Idylla whether she is ruler or consort. So it has been for generations."

"I—" For the first time since he'd met her, Calista Skyros actually looked...rattled. "I can't wear that."

"You must," he said, simply enough. "It is a

symbol. It is meaningful to our people. And it matters to me that it grace the left hand of my bride, as custom and tradition requires."

He watched her swallow, as if her throat hurt. "I think you should save it," she said in a low voice, after a moment. "For someone more appropriate."

"We are far past the point of debating what is *appropriate*." He held the ring in his hand, admiring, as he always did, the ancient workmanship. The pile of diamonds and sapphires, seemingly haphazard, yet all together a monument to sea and sky that captured the essence of his island kingdom. "I do not plan to have a selection of queens, Calista. Only the one."

Her gaze had dropped to the ring he held while he spoke, but she jerked it up to his face then.

"Of course you don't think…" She blinked, and for the first time since they'd met, looked…uncertain. Off balance. "This can't be…"

His head tipped to one side. "Do you know something about my marriage that I do not, Lady Calista?"

And he watched as she took a deep, shaky breath. Then another.

"You are being bullied into this whole thing by my father," she said after a moment. "I assumed the moment you found yourself free of whatever he held over you, you would divorce me or annul this, or whatever it is kings do to rearrange reality to suit themselves."

"Henry VIII preferred execution. Is that what you mean?"

"Surely you don't think this is anything but temporary. You can't."

Orion should rejoice in that, surely. He should have felt relief pouring through him, because their first interaction had been so fraught and this, at last, was some sense. Some acknowledgment of what was happening and even the faintest hint that they might share a bit in this thing that they must do.

But instead, he was caught somewhere between her clever mouth and that odd, arrested expression in her gaze.

And when he shook himself out of that, he reminded himself sternly that it didn't matter if Calista had a modern sensibility about the situation they found themselves in. It couldn't. It changed nothing.

"There will be no divorce," he told her. "No annulment. My father's reign was too tumultuous. Too humiliating and upsetting, for this family and the country. There will be no scandal if I can help it."

If anything, that seemed to agitate her more.

"Your Majesty. Really." She moistened her lip and he found himself drawn to that, too. What was the matter with him? "You can't possibly think that we would suit for anything more than a temporary arrangement to appease my father's worst impulses."

He had been horrified by her earlier. And now he wanted to argue with her about their suitability?

"I need to marry, Lady Calista. I need to produce heirs, and quickly, to prove to my people the kingdom is at last in safe hands. There will be no divorce." He smiled more than he should have, perhaps, when she looked stricken. "We are stuck. In each other's pockets, it seems."

She blanched at that, but he had no pity for her. Or nothing so simple as pity, anyway.

He moved toward her, taking stock of the way she lifted her head too quickly—very much as if she was beating back the urge to leap backward. To scramble away from him, as if he was some kind of predator.

The truth was, something in him roared its approval at that notion. He, who had always prided himself on how civilized he was, did not dislike the idea that here, with her, he was as much a man as any other.

Surely that had to be a good sign for their marriage.

Whether it was or wasn't, he stopped when he reached her. Then he stood before her and took her hand in his.

And the contact, skin on skin, floored him. It was so...*tactile*.

It made him remember the images that had been dancing in his head ever since he'd brought up sex in her presence. It made him imagine it all in intricate detail.

It made him hard and needy, but better yet, it made her tremble.

Very solemnly, he took the ring—the glorious ring that in many ways was Idylla's standard to wave proudly before the world—and slid it onto one of her slender fingers.

And because he was a gentleman and a king, did not point out that she was shaking while he did it.

"And now," he said, in a low voice that should have been smooth, or less harshly possessive, but wasn't, "you are truly my betrothed. The woman who will be my bride. My queen. Your name will be bound to mine for eternity."

"I understand what it means."

But her voice, too, wasn't as sharp as usual. He expected her to yank back her hand, but she didn't. He had the odd notion that she couldn't.

The funny thing was, though he had never imagined that he would be blackmailed into marriage, it was no hardship at all to admit that Lady Calista looked a great deal like the woman he'd always vaguely imagined would be his. She was prettier than the last time he'd seen her, he was sure. There was something ethereal about her tonight, with her hair arranged on top of her head in something that looked effortlessly chic and complicated.

It called attention to the beauty of her bone structure, from her high cheekbones to her elegant nose.

She looked like the queen she would become, and soon.

Orion dropped her hand, and was pleased to see that for a moment, she held hers where it was. Right there in midair, staring at the astounding ring on her hand as if she couldn't quite believe it was real.

When she finally dropped it to her side, she looked almost lost. He told himself that was why he offered her his arm.

And when he led her from the salon, then down through the grand halls of the palace to the car that waited to take them from the palace, she seemed…almost subdued. Uncharacteristically, he would have said.

Though in truth he knew very little about her character—other than the fact she was happy to participate in his blackmail, that was.

"Where are my parents?" she asked when they were both inside the car, and his driver had pulled away from the palace.

"I sent them in a separate vehicle," Orion

said coolly. "Is that a problem? You will understand, I think, if I would prefer to do without your father's company at present."

"My father can be difficult," she agreed, with a small laugh. And something in her gaze that he might have mistaken for dislike, had she been anyone else. Someone who didn't work so closely with Aristotle, for a start.

Orion settled himself in his seat, wishing for perhaps the first time in his life that it was a tighter, smaller car. So that he would have the opportunity to touch her more. To enjoy the fact she was sitting there beside him, smiling faintly of something he could only describe as sparkling vanilla.

"Why do you do his bidding if you find him as difficult as the rest of us do?" he asked, because the seat was vast and it was the only way of touching her available to him.

And he didn't want to investigate why it was he wanted that so much.

It seemed to take her a long moment to lift her gaze from where it rested on her hand in her lap. On the ring she wore. His ring, claiming her.

Something roared in him at that, too.

When her eyes met his, she looked far less dazed than before. And Orion found, to his surprise, that he liked the sharpness. The challenge.

That intensity that was only Calista.

She shook her head. "Of all people to ask me that question."

"I don't follow."

Calista didn't quite laugh. "Don't you? My mistake. Or are you not the man who followed the dictates of a mad king for the better part of his life?"

That was a direct hit, but a part of him enjoyed that she swung at him like that. A part of him wanted more—because whatever else it was, unlike so much else in his life, it was real.

"The difference being that my father was indeed the king. Yours is…what? A businessman with a family title?"

"As if a hereditary king is any different."

"You could leave at any time," Orion pointed out. "You could have stayed in France, for example. Or gone off to America, as so many do. Instead, you chose to stay. Here, on the island. And to involve yourself in his schemes."

She pressed her lips together. "You wouldn't understand."

"Perhaps not. But I do know that I would never participate in blackmail."

But if he expected to shame her, he was disappointed. She only shrugged, then smirked a bit, as if pleased with her own insolence. "That doesn't keep me up at night, Your Majesty. Did you think it would?"

"Orion."

Her smirk faltered. "I beg your pardon?"

It was his turn to shrug, then. "You're my betrothed. And, apparently, intend to continue to treat me in as cavalier a fashion as possible. You might as well use the correct name, don't you think?"

And he could see, somehow, that didn't sit well with her. That there was something about the request that made her shift, then sit even more stiffly beside him.

"That wouldn't be right," she said, glaring

down at the ring on her finger. "That would make everything...messier."

"Would it?" He found himself smiling, and his heart was beating too fast in his chest. "Or is it instead fear? Once you succumb to familiarity, will it be harder and harder to do your father's bidding?"

She let out a breath that was not quite a laugh. "Don't be silly."

"Familiarity. Intimacy. These things take their own toll. What will become of you, Calista, do you think?"

"I didn't give you permission to use *my* name," she pointed out, but there was no heat in it.

They were in the back of a car, winding their way down the hill into the city proper. They were as alone as they could get.

Maybe that was why he reached over and picked up her hand, the hand that wore the ring that was the symbol of his kingdom.

"I am your king," he reminded her. "I do not require your permission. And in any case, using your name is the very least of the intimacies I plan to share with you tonight."

Her gaze flew to his, alarmed. "Tonight? What intimacies?"

"It is customary to seal the announcement of a royal engagement with a kiss, Calista. Surely you know this."

"How would I have the slightest idea?" she asked, her voice sharp again. But not, he rather thought, in quite the same way it had been. Instead, it felt connected to all that heat in him. "I wasn't alive when your father and mother were betrothed, was I? How could I possibly know how they did it?"

"I thought all Idyllian girls were raised on dreams of marrying into the royal family."

Her hand in his flexed, as if she wanted to curl it into a fist. "Not this Idyllian girl."

"My father was more traditional back then," Orion told her. "He was still the crown prince, for one thing, and my grandfather would have taken a dim view of any deviation from tradition. So at the first of the holiday balls, my father presented my mother to the kingdom, as the Kings of Idylla have always done. He showed them all that the ring of Idylla sat on her hand, claiming her for the people as well as himself. And he kissed her on the balcony of the opera house, then danced with her as a grateful nation cheered."

"That sounds ghastly. My teeth hurt just thinking about all that forced sweetness."

"Nevertheless, we will follow the same script. Your dental trauma notwithstanding."

"Will we?" She glared at him. "I have no desire to kiss you, on an opera balcony or anywhere else, and I don't dance."

"Whether you choose to dance or not, in your private life, is your business, Calista." She tried to tug her hand from his, but he held on. "But tonight, your dancing is my business, and I regret to inform you that I'm already well aware that you know how. Like every other girl of noble birth, you were trained in such things at a very young age. Did you think I would not check?"

"You can't make me dance with you."

"I don't have to," Orion said, almost idly. "You appear to be more afraid of your father than you are of me. Feel free to tell him that you intend to buck tradition entirely tonight. I'm sure he will be fully supportive of this choice."

She was silent for a moment. The car was making its way down one of the city's wide boulevards, done up with holiday lights. Flags waved from the hood while people lined the street, the holiday decorations that went up this first week of November making them look red and green and gold, and cheered.

"If you kiss me, I will bite you," Calista promised him.

"Another empty threat, I think." And suddenly, it occurred to Orion that he was enjoying himself. He hardly knew where to put that, so unexpected was it. "But never fear, my surprisingly bashful betrothed. It cannot be a real kiss. That would be inappropriate."

She wrinkled up her nose. "What a relief."

And Orion never surrendered to his demons. He never let feelings control him. Urges were anathema to him and strong emotion was his enemy.

Still, what moved in him then proved too strong to deny.

He reached over and took hold of her, sliding his hand along the curve of her cheek and then guiding her face to his.

"What—? What are you—?"

She sounded breathless. But she didn't pull away.

"This is a real kiss, Calista," he heard himself say.

And then he demonstrated.

CHAPTER FOUR

THE KING WAS kissing her.

And, worse, he was kissing her *well.*

Everything inside Calista went haywire. Alarms kicked off other alarms, each shrieking so loud it should have deafened her completely, but he kept going.

And despite herself, she felt herself...softening.

His lips coaxed hers. His mouth, so stern from a distance, was firm against hers, and it made her stomach dance.

Butterflies, something in her whispered.

She pulled back slightly, perhaps to consider the horror of that thought—

But that was when he angled his head and took the kiss deeper.

And everything inside Calista burst into flame.

It went on and on. She burned, and she kissed him back, moving closer to him as if that would make the fire in her better. Or hotter. She couldn't tell which.

There was a song in her, louder and louder, and it took her a moment to realize when he pulled away. And worse, that her hands were clenched on the fine fabric of his jacket.

For one breath, two, she could only cling to him. And stare back at him, astonished.

But then reality reasserted itself and she hitched in a breath.

"We won't be doing that again," she said, hoping she sounded more outraged and faintly disgusted than what she was. Knocked off balance. At sea, even.

But the way Orion very nearly smiled at her suggested otherwise. He looked far too male. Too smug. She told herself that was redundant and he was a king who was the worst of men anyway, and tried her best to make herself furious—

All while terribly afraid that she was trembling with all that leftover sensation. Visibly.

"If you say so," he murmured. In a dark, rich tone that should not have had anything to do with the sensation of sparks cascading down her spine. She managed not to shudder. Somehow.

And it took the concentrated force of all her willpower, far more than it should have, but she managed to keep from pressing her fingers to her lips. Because it suddenly seemed to her like an act of sheer survival to prevent him from knowing how much he'd affected her.

No matter how much of a lost cause that might have been. It was one thing for him to suspect. But if he knew…

Well. She didn't intend to let that happen.

And no matter that she could still taste him in her mouth.

Orion reached into his jacket pocket and pulled out his mobile, more evidence that his royal blood did not prevent him from being a mortal man like anyone else. Like everyone else, even. She pretended not to watch him scrolling through whatever messages waited him with an expression that was entirely too calm for her tastes.

Surely if she felt wrecked, torn inside out and made new despite herself, he should feel the same. And it should show.

But Calista had turned biting her tongue into an art, or she never would have survived her childhood, and she did it now. She jerked her gaze away from Orion. She folded her hands in her lap, maneuvering around the unfamiliar ring that sat on her hand, so beautiful she didn't dare look at directly. And yet heavy enough to feel like a portable dungeon.

She directed her gaze out the window instead, at the royal city that slipped by as the car took them toward this destiny of hers that she had never wanted.

This destiny she had felt fairly smug about until tonight, if she was honest. Before he'd kissed her. Before he'd taken her mouth with such raw, consuming mastery that she still felt fluttery, knocked off balance, and a little silly.

And Calista had no experience whatsoever with *silly*. She hardly knew what to do with herself.

Especially when Orion appeared to expect this union of theirs to be permanent.

"I hope you're prepared," Orion said from beside her, surprising her. Once again, his voice went off inside her like a tuning fork and everything in her yearned toward him, like a song.

She would cut out her own tongue before she gave in and actually sang, thank you very much. She promised herself that no matter what, she would ignore that odd urge.

Calista cleared her throat. She felt almost misshapen, as if he'd kissed her so thoroughly that if she were to look in a mirror just now, she wouldn't recognize her own face. She didn't test that theory.

"What sort of preparation do you mean?" she asked, as smoothly as she could, and congratulated herself on sounding anything but shaken up. "I'm the vice president at a multinational corporation, but thank you. I don't normally need to be reminded to prepare for a party."

"I cannot speak to corporate wrangling, of course," Orion said. With a glint in those grave eyes of his that she was tempted to consider evidence of a heretofore unknown sense of humor in the new, stern king. Surely not, she thought. Her head must still be spinning. "Or party planning, for that matter. But you must know that the moment you emerge from this vehicle on my arm, your life will change."

She waited for him to laugh. Or even smirk. He didn't.

And she felt herself go cold. "What do you mean by that? I don't want my life to change. I like my life." Or she would soon enough, anyway. "I've worked hard on the life I have."

With single-minded focus, in fact. All pushing toward the finish line she could finally— *finally*—see before her.

But the cheers from outside the car seemed to press in on her, then. The way the city slid by as if it, too, danced attendance on this man. Then again, maybe it was the way he studied her expression, the look on his face a bit too close to pity for her liking.

"Surely you cannot be so naive," Orion said, and the fact that his tone was gentle kept her still.

So still it prevented her from snapping at him, or even getting her back up in the first place. Both of which she would have preferred, because the alternative was staring back at him, feeling awfully close to stricken.

"Every time I escort a woman to an event,

it is like a feeding frenzy," he told her in the same way. Kind enough. Gentle, too. But certain all the same. "No matter how many times I tell them that the women in question are my poor cousins, the result is the same. A complete and utter circus."

She knew all about that circus. She'd seen enough of it without even looking for it—on the television, in all the newsagents. She'd even known, the way everyone did, that if Orion had ever dated, he'd managed to keep it quiet.

She'd known all of that in the way she knew what month Christmas was. Or that snow was cold, little though it fell in Idylla. It wasn't anything personal, it was just a fact.

Her heart squeezed tight in her chest, then began to beat like a drum.

He continued to eye her with that mix of pity and patience. "But I have never before arrived at one of the holiday balls with a woman I was not related to, Calista. You should prepare yourself, at the very least, for the reaction the crowd will have when you exit the car."

"But… But I…"

But Orion wasn't finished. And worse, he seemed inclined to keep sounding kind, which was the last thing Calista wanted. It made everything so much harder.

It made her feel so much weaker.

"All of that will pale in comparison to the fervor that will grip the nation, the press, and a good part of the world once we announce that our engagement is finally going ahead tonight, all these years after my father arranged it." His voice was as grave as his expression, then. And the small gleam she saw in his eyes had nothing to do with amusement, she was sure. "I do hope you know what you've gotten yourself into."

For a moment she didn't know what he meant. Then she remembered. Blackmail. Her vile, grasping father and this thing she'd become to counter him. To fight him—all while appearing to have surrendered to him long ago. All to save her sister no matter the cost to herself.

Her throat was so dry she thought it might catch fire.

"I'll be fine," she replied, though her lips still felt stung and stained from his. Her pulse had taken on a hectic life of its own, and the noise from outside the car as it began to slow in its final approach to the opera house seemed to batter against her.

Like real blows.

Orion reached over and took her hand. For a moment her heart seemed to seize inside her chest. But instead of lacing his fingers with hers or caressing her in some way—which she assured herself she would have shaken off at once—he fiddled with the ring he'd put there instead. It was the ring of the Queens of Idylla, after all. Every school-aged child knew that and could identify it on sight.

What they didn't, couldn't know was that the ring itself was warm against her skin. Or that the stones caught the light from the street outside, sending fragments and patches of illumination dancing about in a shimmering splendor.

The light caught his profile, too. The same profile that would soon grace the Idyllian currency, slowly taking his father's place. He looked like precisely what and who he was, the product of centuries of royal blood. As if the throne of Idylla was superimposed on his skin.

That should have horrified her, surely.

But it didn't.

And when he didn't speak, his fingers on that ring as if that was all the statement necessary, Calista felt as if the bottom of the car fell out from underneath her. As if she was suddenly tossed out into the cobbled streets, unable to gain purchase or find her feet or even *breathe.*

The chanting and cheering outside grew louder. And she knew no one could see her inside the car, with its tinted, no doubt armored windows. But even so, she couldn't seem to make her lungs work the way they were supposed to. And she felt dizzy all over again, but this time it was from nothing so pleasant as a kiss.

Because it hadn't occurred to her until this very moment that as fake as she wanted to treat their engagement, or even their marriage, that was the private reality. That was what was between them because they knew the truth of things.

But there was going to be a huge public reality she couldn't control.

Calista had been so busy focusing on how best to ignore the whole marriage thing while she pursued her own ends that she'd neglected to think about what it was going to mean to announce herself engaged or even adjacent to... Orion Augustus Pax. The bloody king.

Her attitude in that private salon the day she'd first met him struck her, then, as hilariously idiotic. If not actively suicidal.

The truth was, she wasn't a public person. Her father was notorious, and that was about as much public attention as she'd ever wanted. It had led to snide comments at school. The odd sharp word. But mostly, the many people her father offended went after him, not her.

Unlike many of her peers, Calista wasn't the sort who constantly had her picture in the society pages. Nor did she parade about Europe, from yacht to club to charity ball. She had always been too busy working. And the irony wasn't lost on her that her life's work was in a media company that existed almost entirely because it procured pictures of others and made them public whether they wanted those moments shared or not.

Maybe because of the things Skyros Media had done, Calista had always preferred to stay behind the scenes.

She felt herself begin to sweat as the car rolled to a stop.

Outside, there was a loud, endless roll of noise, like the wall-sized swells at sea. She tried to make herself breathe, but she couldn't seem to get any air much deeper than the back of her throat.

"Is it always like this?" she managed to ask. Faintly.

"I am the king," Orion replied, mildly enough, though she had the feeling those grave hazel eyes saw far too much of her internal battle. "Better they should greet me with expressions of joy than the howls of hatred they used to greet my father. Don't you think?"

"I was never the sort of person who chased around after the royal motorcade," she made herself say in a sharper sort of voice, though she was still but a shadow of her usual self.

"So I can't say I ever paid much attention to the cacophony one way or another."

He only looked at her. Until she couldn't tell whether the noise outside was the crowd or if it was inside her, somehow. As if it was part of that singing thing that seemed to connect them, heating as it sang, until she felt scalded straight through. Or maybe she had already been scalded, her skin stripped away so she *felt* too much, despite her best efforts. Maybe one royal kiss had rewired her brain—by burning it up into ash and need and noise.

Or maybe you need to get a hold of yourself, she told herself sharply. *This whole thing is nothing but a distraction.*

"Isn't this where you tell me I don't have to do this if I don't want to?" she asked before she thought better of it.

His mouth firmed then, forming a hard, stern line. And she couldn't decide if she found that comforting or insulting, but it didn't matter.

Because the look in his eyes matched the shape of his mouth and pinned her to her seat.

"But that is the rub, is it not? You do have to do this. As do I. That is the nature of black-

mail, I think you'll find. So tawdry and re-
volting. One is ever forced to do detestable
things."

Pull yourself together now, Calista ordered
herself. *It's only a crowd. And he's only a
man. A very powerful, very pampered man.*

Though this close to Orion, Calista couldn't
help but think he didn't feel like *only* anything.

Maybe it was nerves that kept her mouth
going. "At the very least I would have thought
you'd have sage advice to offer. That I should
imagine them all naked, or something."

"I can't imagine I would find the prospect
of a heaving mass of nudity particularly comforting," King Orion said, his voice dark and
sardonic. And possibly *satisfied*, too. "But
if that helps you, Calista, then by all means.
Imagine whatever sea of flesh you think will
make you calm."

She stared out the window for another moment, still feeling stricken and breathless.
And hopelessly out of her depth. Then she
blinked. "You're right. That's not better at
all."

Orion fixed her with another long, dark

stare. He didn't say another word, but still, she could feel the weight of the way he regarded her. As if it had its own heft and heavy, booted feet.

He rapped on his window, and a moment later, the door was opened. The roar from outside shoved in, even louder and wilder. He flicked Calista a look, indicating that she should slide after him to exit behind him.

Then he stepped out—into the noise, the lights, and the howls as they greeted him—with an innate athleticism that made her blink.

This was a fine moment indeed to rethink her choices. A fine moment to ask herself why she hadn't pushed back a bit harder against her father. It was hard to remember why she'd chosen to go along with all this nonsense as she sat here in the back of a royal vehicle, her last moments as a private citizen spiraling away from her. It was hard to remember anything, really—much less all the reasons she'd had for allowing her father to think he was still in control of her.

The one very good reason in particular.

She could hear a strange little sound, high-pitched and plainly terrified, and realized she was panting.

And as she didn't wish her big moment in the spotlight to coincide with the first time she fainted, she made herself take a deep breath. Then another.

Outside the car, in the wedge between door and vehicle, she could see Orion waving at the crowd. At his subjects. And what was left of her time was ticking away, second by second.

She reminded herself this was a distraction from her plan, not the plan itself.

And she reminded herself that none of this mattered. What mattered was surviving it intact so she could do what *she* wanted to do. Orion was being blackmailed. Calista was simply doing what was expedient.

Orion turned slightly, extending his hand back into the vehicle.

She didn't lie and tell herself that wasn't a sovereign command, because she knew it was.

God help her, but she wasn't ready. She hadn't thought this through. It had been one thing to sit in a private room in the palace and shoot off her mouth, but this was something else. This was terrifying.

She was *terrified*.

Orion waited with a kind of brooding, intense patience, his hand extended.

Calista found herself mute, frozen, and lost all the same in that grave gaze he settled on her.

Every inch of him a king. Her king. There was no doubt that the way he looked at her was an order from on high.

And on some distant level, she was astonished to find that it worked. She couldn't seem to grasp onto a full thought in her head, but her body obeyed him anyway. She was moving automatically, reaching out to grasp his hand, like a deep, blooming flame when his strong fingers closed around hers.

For an eternity, there was only that. The flame and the bloom of it, eating her whole. His hand in hers. And the way their eyes caught, her still in the shadows of the car and him outside.

Her heart seemed to wallop her inside her own chest, like it was a weapon, and worse, he wielded it.

And then everything sped up.

Orion helped her alight from the car in another smooth, easy show of strength, though Calista rather thought it looked like nothing more than good manners. She tucked that away, because the fact the king was built like a god felt like a burst of sunshine deep inside her.

There was a smile on his face as he greeted her, though perhaps only she could see it didn't match the intensity of the way he looked at her.

"Optics, my lady," he murmured near her ear as he brushed a cool kiss across her cheek, and then he turned.

Presenting her to the crowd.

And sealing her fate, which felt a lot like drowning.

For a long while, possibly an intertwined string of forevers, there was nothing but the endless noise. Bright lights, popping flashbulbs, disorienting and overwhelming.

But Orion never let go of her. And Calista held on to her smile and his strong hand as if her life depended on it.

She rather thought it did.

And by the time they made it up the red-carpeted aisle to the ornate front doors of the Royal Opera House, where the inaugural holiday ball was always held, Calista felt as if she'd run back-to-back marathons. She, who had never deliberately run more than a few feet in her life.

If this was what it felt like, panicked and distraught down to her very bones, she had no plans to start.

Inside the first vestibule of the opera house, it was shockingly quiet. So quiet that it almost hurt.

Except, of course, for the ragged sound of her breathing.

"Try not to hyperventilate," Orion advised her, in that same mild way of his that was simultaneously enraging and comforting. "This is the opera, I grant you. But even so, best to avoid the fainting couch. It will only raise unfortunate questions."

"I'm perfectly fine," she managed to say, though she wasn't. She really, really wasn't. But as she didn't plan to collapse on the floor and cry, what was the point of saying so?

"I'm delighted to hear it."

Orion nodded past her. That was when it occurred to Calista to look around, too. Beneath the dramatic gargoyles up high and statuary littered about the marble foyer, there were liveried servants standing at the ready.

And she realized what she should already have known. Most people did not get a moment to collect themselves before entering the ball proper. This was an indulgence granted the king, no doubt so he could make an appropriately pageant-like entrance.

So that *they* could make an entrance, she corrected herself. Together.

Because this was what she'd signed up for. Or her father had signed her up for, which amounted to the same thing. And it was no one's fault but hers that she'd failed to think it through.

Calista blew out a breath, found her smile again, and took the arm he offered her.

And then, like it or not, she allowed the King of Idylla to walk her into the first holiday ball of the season.

Worse still, she allowed him to claim her as his with a perfect, romantic kiss from the balcony that would have swept her off her feet entirely. That would have made her forget the crowd, and the astonishment from all quarters, and the cruel satisfaction on her father's face.

It would have broken her heart and sewed it back together, she was sure, if only she hadn't been faking.

And if she had to remind herself, repeatedly, that she was faking, that Orion was performing under duress, that none of this was real nor ever could be—

Well.

Calista had learned a long time ago how to keep a smile on her face and pretend like her life depended on it. Like Melody's life depended on it, too.

Because it always had.

CHAPTER FIVE

"THE STAFF IS in disarray," Griffin declared, letting himself into Orion's study.

"Do come in, Griffin," Orion murmured sardonically as his brother prowled over to fling himself in his favorite chair, without even pretending to wait for an invitation. "Make yourself right at home. No need to worry I might be tending to delicate matters of state."

He wasn't, just at the moment. But he certainly could have been.

Griffin looked notably unbothered at the possibility. "It's an uproar out there. The palace halls are alive with speculation now that everything has been made official and all the rumors are at an end. You may have kicked off a revolution after all."

Orion sighed and stopped attempting to make sense of the latest lengthy, meandering tome that his least favorite minister had presented him, expecting Orion would have it read and annotated with cogent commentary already. He rubbed at his temples, suddenly aware that he'd been at his desk reading stacks upon stacks of documents since early that morning. Because like it or not, he was playing catch-up on the past twenty years. The whole of his father's reign.

"What is it I've done to provoke the revolutionary forces today?" He eyed his younger brother with the usual mix of baffled affection, no little hint of jealousy at the antics Griffin as spare rather than heir was permitted to get up to, and a rush of gratitude that all the same, they were who they were.

"Your fiancée, my liege," Griffin drawled, stretching out his legs. He was dressed for appointments, though he preferred a rather more carefree and rumpled approach to his sartorial choices. Then again, no one expected any different from a man not expected to ever take the throne. "Or are you unaware that she has refused to submit herself to the tender ministrations of your fleet of private secretaries?"

"What do they want from Calista?" Orion

asked, and couldn't help but think that it was an excellent question. One he asked himself nightly, come to that.

He kept waiting for familiarity to breed contempt, as it was meant to do. But instead, the more time he spent with the woman he was to marry, the more feverish his nights became. Because the more he saw her, the more he wanted her.

It hadn't helped that he'd seen beneath that sharp, edgy surface she wore so comfortably. He could have done without the vulnerability she'd shown before their first ball. Just like he could have happily stayed ignorant of the way she tasted.

It would have made things easier, surely.

During the long nights when all he did was ache for her, he reminded himself that finding himself sexually attracted to a woman he was forced to marry anyway was a gift. That he should celebrate it, no matter how the marriage itself came to be. Because that attraction could only make what lay ahead of the pair of them easier. More pleasant, certainly.

During the day, however, he reminded himself whose daughter she was. And he was horrified that he was allowing the chemistry between them to poison him, when he knew better.

Of course he knew better.

Every week, he collected her from the same salon. She wore a series of exquisite ensembles, all of which were gushed over and picked apart the following day in all the papers, much the way their engagement kiss had been. And not only in the ones her family owned.

There had been no more kissing. No more fraught conversations laced with need. And no more flashes of vulnerability, for that matter.

Instead, they danced.

And it did not help Orion in the slightest to discover that Calista Skyros—blackmailer's daughter, insolent and disrespectful by nature and inclination alike—fit him like all those steamy dreams he had. Graceful. Lithe. Something like ethereal.

As if she had been specifically created to fit right there in his arms.

When that could not possibly be true. He knew it wasn't true.

And in case he thought he was imagining such things, no. He'd seen the pictures of the two of them. He could hardly have avoided them if he'd wanted to. And worse, the videos that made it clear their chemistry was not only in his head.

God help him.

"They want Calista to act the way the king's betrothed ought to act," Griffin was saying. He shook his head at his older brother, and Orion opted not to let himself notice the speculative gleam in Griffin's gaze. "It is all so irregular, after all. She has refused to present herself for the proper... How shall I put it? Molding."

"She dances as a girl of noble blood ought to have learned as a child. She wears appropriate clothing and has yet to embarrass the palace. What else should she be doing?"

"Come now, brother." Griffin laughed. "Surely you have not already forgotten the greatest joy of our formative years? Day after day after day of royal etiquette pounded into our heads by battalions of grandfather's private secretaries?"

Orion opted not to mention that he had enjoyed those sessions rather more than Griffin had. "Again, Lady Calista is of noble blood, born and raised right here in Idylla. I have it on the greatest authority that she has already suffered through comportment classes. At length."

Griffin only shrugged. "I'm not the one who needs convincing. I don't much care. It's your staff, Orion. They believe your chosen bride is…" He paused, then, in a manner that Orion might have called *delicate* had he not been able to see the smirk on his brother's face. "…too well versed in playing to the press. While ignorant of the duties that await her once she marries you."

Orion accepted the fact that he did not particularly want to deal with the endlessly thorny problem that was Calista. But when he glanced down at the sheaves upon sheaves of papers on his desk, it seemed less overwhelming a task than it might have otherwise.

Liar, something in him whispered. *You* want *to deal with her. You want to see her when you know you shouldn't.*

He stood, inclining his head grandly at Griffin—who only grinned back, sprawled out with every appearance of idleness. "Thank you for bringing this to my attention. I am forced to wonder why I employ a staff at all when they are more comfortable gossiping to my younger brother than bringing their concerns straight to me."

"It is more that I like to gossip, as I think you know," Griffin said mildly. "What else is Idylla's favorite playboy to do with his fortune and time?"

Orion smoothed a hand down the pristine front of the suit he wore. "About that."

"Yes, yes," Griffin said, rolling his eyes. "I haven't forgotten what I promised you."

"If you do not choose a bride for yourself, brother," Orion said quietly, "you may force me into a position where I must choose for you. Is that what you want?"

Griffin didn't look remotely concerned. "Father chose your bride. You seem to be holding up well."

"If by that you mean I am acquitting myself with all magnificence of my station, yes. That is my job."

"You don't look at her like she's a *job*,

Orion." Griffin flashed another grin when Orion glared at him, and shrugged. "You don't. And who on this planet knows more about carrying the sins of the fathers than you and me? Perhaps this girl—"

"I understand my duty, Griffin." Orion sounded harsher than he meant to, especially where his brother was involved. Given Griffin only ever looked delighted that he'd provoked a reaction—any reaction. Today was no different. "And I will do my duty, as always. You may recall you promised me that you would do the same."

"My problem isn't finding one woman to marry, Orion," Griffin said then, his grin so bright it almost concealed the darker gleam in his gaze that Orion sometimes thought only he ever saw. "It's that there are far too many to wade through, all with their own particular demands."

"I'm happy to do it for you, then, if you find the task too onerous."

"Perhaps you should deal with your recalcitrant bride-to-be," Griffin suggested, laughing. "I'll find my own, don't you worry."

Orion did worry. He worried about everything, the way he always had—because there was no one else to do it. But he knew there was no pressing Griffin when he was in one of his languid moods, so Orion left him in his office and marched out to find his staff, half expecting to find that Griffin had misread the situation. More than half. Because sometimes it was hard to tell what was actually gossip swirling about the palace, and what Griffin decided to make gossip.

But when he astonished his staff by presenting himself in their offices, everyone leaped to their feet and began bowing dramatically. And in the resulting chaos, he quickly understood that for once, his brother had not been exaggerating.

"Her behavior is quite extraordinary," his head secretary confided once they'd left the bowing and scraping behind and repaired to the man's office, where he looked ill at the sight of his sovereign sitting in a regular chair in front of the desk. But he pressed on. "In the history of the throne, there has never been a queen who…" He blinked, as if he could hardly bring himself to say the word. "Your Majesty, Lady Calista *works*."

"In her family firm, yes. I believe she's quite proud of this."

His secretary managed to radiate severe disapproval while looking faintly obsequious. A skill Orion doubted he could master. But he was too busy wondering when he'd appointed himself Calista's champion to study how the other man did it.

"The wedding will be on Christmas Eve, sire," his secretary pointed out.

"I have not forgotten."

His secretary bent his head. "And your fiancée has yet to present herself at the palace so that we can begin to instruct her in the duties of her new role. She cannot…simply *appear* overnight and hope to acquit herself as queen. That would be disastrous."

Orion did not need his secretary to remind him that there had been enough disasters in the kingdom already. His staff had been forced to help him through his father's rule, where they'd spent their days attempting to smooth everything out, fix what was fixable, and do their best to present the public with a vision of a better, calmer, more competent king than the one they had.

Of course they were all concerned that his fiancée represented a kind of throwback to those chaotic years.

Still.

"It is not as if she's a stranger we picked up off the streets," Orion pointed out, a bit drily. "She is the daughter of Idyllian nobility."

"Which has no doubt prepared her adequately for a robust role as a socialite, Your Majesty, but can in no way substitute for proper training in how to represent the kingdom as its queen. That is, as they say, a different kettle of fish entirely."

Despite himself, Orion found himself thinking about his own mother. She had received all that same instruction, presumably. But she'd been so young. And no one could have been instructed in what it took to handle his father. Especially given what Orion knew now, it was perhaps unsurprising that his mother had taken her own life in the end.

He thought of the stark terror he'd seen on Calista's face in the car that first night. That hint that she was something more than simply her odious father's daughter, sent to enact his squalid little games.

And the thought that another queen—*his* queen—might end up in such despair that she followed in his mother's sad footsteps one day made something in him shift. Hard. As if the notion might take him from his feet.

"Leave it with me," he told his secretary.

And then he decided to indulge himself while he was off putting out fires.

His father had dearly loved the pageant of monarchy. Always a motorcade. A parade, if possible. Armed guards wherever he went and as much pomp and circumstance as every engagement could hold.

And pageantry had its place, certainly. Orion tried to be careful not to eschew things simply because his father had enjoyed them—like the glorious history of the throne of Idylla, and of his family.

But today, Orion changed into regular clothes and slipped out a side door of the palace where reporters were never allowed to camp out and wait. He would have loved to have gone alone, but he was a king, and well aware of his responsibilities—even when he was shirking them. And so two bodyguards came with him, also dressed down, though they fanned out enough to give him the illusion of living a normal enough life that he could simply…take a walk in the royal city if he liked.

And he did like. Every now and again, he liked to go out from the palace and away from his usual concerns and blend in. Sometimes his subjects recognized him, but they were usually so delighted to see the king out there engaging in normal pursuits—instead of making embarrassing headlines like his father had—that they rarely caused a fuss.

Today, it was a brisk morning. Cool, by Mediterranean standards. Orion followed a meandering sort of path down the hill where the palace sat, a beacon of depravity or hope, depending on how well he was doing his job. He found his way into the affluent part of the city, where the better part of Idyllian nobility lived while in town. He knew they all had their ancestral estates either out in the rural parts of the main island, or on the smaller, supplementary islands that made up the rest of the kingdom.

As he drew close to the street where Calista lived in her father's grand old house, he slowed, because he could see the scrum of paparazzi from a distance. They heaved about outside Aristotle Skyros's house, even though, as far as Orion could see, there was no one there to take pictures of.

He didn't turn down the street. Why give the vultures more to pick apart? He kept walking, flipping up his collar against the damp as he made his way into the central business district.

And once again, he saw paparazzi six deep, milling around outside Skyros Media's flagship building.

After a brief consultation with his bodyguards, he let them lead him around to the back, down an alley where he slipped in a heavy door that was marked Exit Only.

He jogged up the stairs to the third floor, where he'd been told Calista's office was, thinking he would drop in on his lovely fiancée for a little chat she wouldn't have had time to prepare for. He was imagining her reaction to that, sharp and exhilarating, when he stepped into the hallway. And then stopped, because he heard raised voices from around the corner.

"This is not a request, Calista. Have you looked out in the street lately? It's a zoo!"

Orion knew that voice. Aristotle, sounding more vicious and bombastic than usual.

"Papa. Please." Her voice was strained. "I can't abandon my work!"

"Vice presidents grow on trees like olives, girl. You're going to marry the king. That is far more important."

He could have revealed himself, then. He could have marched around the corner and let them know he was there, eavesdropping.

But Orion stayed where he was. Which was how he knew, beyond a shadow of a doubt, that he was not as upright and honorable as he'd always like to imagine he was. Because if he was, he would never stand there and listen as they discussed him and his upcoming marriage. If he was truly a man of honor he would let them know that he could hear their conversation.

He and his bodyguards exchanged a long glance, but none of them moved.

Orion was as surprised as anyone that it turned out he was human, after all.

"That's not a career, is it?" Calista snapped.

"That's a vanity project. *Your* vanity project, not mine."

And the sound of the slap Skyros delivered was still resounding in the air as Orion moved. Without meaning to.

But he had to see it with his own eyes. That red handprint on Calista's cheek and her wide eyes.

Both father and daughter looked stunned to see him as he rounded the corner, but he couldn't take any particular pleasure in that.

Not when he was too busy trying to keep his hands from bunching into fists.

"You do know, Skyros," he managed to say, with what he felt was admirable calm, "that there are penalties for striking a member of the royal family? It's an ancient law, handed down across centuries. But whether or not the nation still likes a hanging, it is illegal to put your hands on any one of us. Treasonous, in point of fact."

So was blackmailing kings, of course, which hadn't given Skyros a moment's pause.

"Where the hell did you come from?" Aristotle barked.

But Calista, Orion noted as he bore down

on them, only held a palm to her bright red cheek, and glared.

At him, not her father.

"Do not put your hands on my fiancée," Orion growled at Skyros. "Or I swear to you, I will see you in chains."

"You wouldn't like the consequences," Aristotle sneered at him. "Mark my words."

"Shall we try it and see?" Orion retorted.

Aristotle only sneered again, then curled his lip at Calista. "My decision stands, girl. You're fired and that's final."

And even though she made a strangled kind of sound at that, as if he'd truly hurt her, Aristotle ignored her. He stormed away, heading toward what Orion assumed was the rest of the Skyros Media offices.

"Did he hurt you?" Orion asked, aware only then that his heart was kicking at him, as if he'd been sprinting for time.

"He slapped me," Calista said brusquely. She dropped her hands from her face—her pretty, lovely face—one red, angry cheek with Aristotle's handprint all too visible. Orion felt something roll over in him, like a fault line about to blow. "He's never shy to dole out a slap or two, if that's what you're asking. I'm just out of practice. I've managed to avoid getting smacked for a long while now. And you turning up here like this doesn't help anything."

"Calista." There were so many things he wanted to say. Too many things, and he could see her stiffening, as if she knew what they might be. So he looked down his nose at her instead. "You forget yourself. I am your sovereign. I go where I like."

"The balls, the dresses, all that king and queen malarkey—" She shook her head, a hectic kind of light in the gaze she trained on him. "None of that has any place here. This is a corporation. People *work* here."

"But not you," Orion pointed out, perhaps not as kindly as he could have. "Or did I misinterpret the fact that your father just fired you?"

He saw something wash over her, some strong emotion that wasn't as simple as her temper. "He's overwrought. He'll come around."

"As it happens, I don't want him to come around." He inclined his head as if he was inviting comment, when he wasn't. "I would prefer it if you didn't work."

She blinked, then scowled at him. "What is that supposed to mean? Did you plan this with him?"

"I do not 'make plans' with a man like your father, Calista. His plans hijacked my own. But as it happens, my staff has been agitating—"

"All your staff does is agitate," she snapped at him. Interrupting him, which made his bodyguards bristle, but at this point he rather thought that was an endearment on her part. Or as close as he would get. "They've been harassing me for weeks."

"It's their job to prepare you for your new role. A job they cannot do if you are here, doing your old one."

Now that his temper was cooling a little, and he was no longer tempted to take a swing at Aristotle, he was able to take in everything else. The way she looked, cool and blonde and untouchable, there in the stark-white hallway. He did not spend a great deal of time surrounded by corporate fashions, but it was instantly clear to him that Calista was dressed to send a specific message.

A message he quite liked.

The high, dangerously sharp heels. The miles of her legs exposed beneath the tailored skirt she wore. Her blouse that managed to hint at her figure while showing none of it, and the soft wrap at her shoulders he shied away from calling a cardigan when it looked far more like an elegant piece of feminine armor. Her hair, as usual, was caught back in something sleek—and his enduring trial was that he liked it. He liked all of it. He liked the way Calista vibrated with tension and intelligence. He liked how tough she looked, if a man knew where to look.

He did.

Corporate life clearly suited her. He felt a pang of regret that she was going to have to step away from it—and then reminded himself that she was the one who had crowed over the fact that he was supposedly in her pocket.

She was still a blackmailer's daughter, sent to do his nefarious bidding.

Why did he struggle to remember that?

"I agreed to marry you," she said, looking as dangerous as her shoes. She folded her arms over her chest and glared at him. "I didn't agree to be hounded by your staff. Or to be fired from my job. Or to have packs of reporters hounding me day and night, while we're on the topic."

"What did you imagine marrying a king would entail?" he asked quietly. Not exactly roughly. "Did you truly believe that the Queen of Idylla would have a day job, Calista? Punch a time card and live for Fridays?"

Her mouth fell open. Orion had the distinct impression that he'd shocked her, and he was reminded, somehow, of her panic the night of their first ball.

"Explain to me how that would work," he suggested, mildly enough. "Your colleagues would be going home as usual while you head to the palace."

"But…"

"It is obvious that it cannot be," he said, when she only gaped at him. "I must tell you, Calista, I don't think you really thought this through. That is a pity, and I do feel for your predicament, but I'm afraid it will not help you any."

"That sounds like a threat."

"Only if you wish it to be."

He wanted to touch her. He didn't know how he didn't. How he kept from running his fingers over her overbright, faintly swollen cheek. How he had managed to convince himself that he was coming here to help when the truth was, he'd only wanted the excuse to be near her again. Who was he fooling?

"I wish my father had never…"

She was wise enough not to finish that sentence. And Orion's smile felt strange on his face. Misshapen, perhaps.

"I wish the same thing," he told her, aware as he said it that it was no longer quite as true as it had been. No longer as true as it *should have* been. He would have to deal with that at some point, too. But her eyes were the color of the sea in summer, and it turned out he was far weaker than he'd ever imagined. "Still, we are here despite our wishes. And I will be moving you into the palace where you belong. Today."

CHAPTER SIX

"I DON'T KNOW what you're going on about," Calista's younger sister, Melody, said in her usually practical, matter-of-fact way. "Not only would I very much like to live in a palace, I would consider it a lovely holiday away from our father."

Most of Calista's things were packed. Her mother had overseen that personally—mostly so she could veto anything she didn't feel was appropriate for the next Queen of Idylla—and Calista had left her to it. There was no arguing with Appollonia when she was in what Melody called her *royalist fugue*.

All that was left was the library. Calista had to content herself with sneaking a few of her favorite books into a satchel, muttering angrily about her fate all the while.

As ever, Melody was unsympathetic.

Calista glared at her, hoping that Melody really could feel other people's gazes on her skin like knives as she liked to claim. Sure enough, her sister smiled. She was sitting cross-legged in her favorite armchair, over near the great fire that Calista had personally made certain was lit each day. It wasn't as if their parents spent any time in this library. Aristotle and Appollonia Skyros didn't have time to *read* when there were worlds to ruin and monarchies to worship.

This library had been installed in the house because libraries were expected in the stately houses of Idylla. Calista and Melody had claimed it ages ago and it had been theirs alone, the two of them.

Calista had hated her time in her father's house, and she and Melody had told each other their complicated, glorious daydreams about getting out of this house. Getting away from him. Getting to live as they liked, far away from here.

But now that it was happening, notably not as planned, she felt hollow inside.

"I don't understand any of this, to be honest," Melody continued, clearly choosing to ignore Calista's mood the way she often did. "I'd love to be a queen. Who wouldn't?

Mother was carrying on about all the dresses and the jewels, but I think I'd enjoy the power."

"The Queen of Idylla is a consort, not a ruler," Calista snapped.

And she curled her hand tight over the jewel she wore. The astonishing jewel King Orion had placed there himself that she should have wrenched off and tossed back at him at the first opportunity.

Instead, to her great shame, she had yet to take it off.

Not even once.

"The consort of the ruler is still closer to being the ruler than we are," Melody pointed out. "I'd take it in a heartbeat."

She did not add: *But I've never been asked.* She didn't have to add it. They both knew full well how their father felt about the daughter he seemed to think had been born blind purely to spite him.

"You should come with me," Calista said fiercely. "I don't feel right about leaving you here. We both know what could happen. It's already bad enough with the minders he keeps hiring to bully you."

But when Melody shrugged, Calista wasn't surprised.

"Then it happens. Of the two of us, Calista, I'm a little more at peace with my fate. And my prospects, such as they are. You don't understand that there's a freedom in being ignored and underestimated."

"You shouldn't have to be at peace with anything. You shouldn't have to be stuck here, either, constantly under threat of being shipped off to some institution if you displease our father—"

"You went to university," Melody said, though she was grinning. "Really, if you think about it, what's the difference?"

Calista tossed her favorite Jane Austen collection into her bag, which was already pushing her capacity to lift, much less carry. There was no point arguing with Melody when she was in this mood. She knew that. Her sister was the last person on this earth who would ever think of herself as a victim, and there was no use trying to convince her otherwise. Still, she couldn't quite get her head around what it would mean for her sister to live here unsupervised with their parents and the questionable aides he insisted loom about the place to "help" with Melody.

Nothing good.

And if her parents made good on the threats they liked to make about shipping Melody away—*To find her true potential,* Aristotle sometimes said, when what he meant was, *Where her existence can no longer plague and shame me*—it would break Calista's heart. Because she knew, even if Melody pretended not to, that the three years Calista had spent in Paris pretending she'd never heard of Idylla or Skyros Media bore no resemblance to the life Melody would lead if their parents succeeded in institutionalizing her.

But it was as if Melody could read all of Calista's thoughts and feelings in the air between them. She stood up from her chair, then came over. She took Calista's shoulders in her hands and held them there. Tightly.

And it was a good thing to remember that Melody was no wilting violet. Her hands were tough. Strong.

So is she, Calista told herself. *And if you don't trust her to take care of herself, are you any better than our parents?*

"Go," Melody said, gently but firmly. "You could even try enjoying yourself, for a change."

Calista blew out a breath, fighting to steady herself against a wave of emotion she couldn't afford. And shouldn't have had in the first place, as this was all a great farce. She wasn't *really* leaving her childhood home to go live with her husband-to-be, who happened to be the king. This wasn't a real engagement and it wouldn't be a real marriage. Why should she suffer real emotions?

She was still on the board. Her plan was still in place whether she went to the office or not. Her revenge—and Melody's freedom—was within reach.

"Enjoy myself?" She tried to laugh. She tried to stop *feeling.* "You do know where I'm going, don't you? I've been fired from my job and now I have to go play pretty princesses." She wanted to make an immature gagging sound, but restrained herself. "I will likely die, Melody, stifled to death by boredom and inactivity."

"You've been working feverishly, day and night, since you were eighteen. I don't think that learning how to be a queen sounds particularly boring, if I'm honest, but even if it is—it has to be more entertaining than spending the whole of your life figuring out ways to thwart Father."

"I don't want to thwart Father," Calista said softly. "I want to destroy him."

And that was just a start.

Melody smiled. "And you will. But I don't see why you wouldn't look at all the avenues available to you now. Instead of the one you decided on when you thought it was the only one around."

Wouldn't that be lovely? Calista entertained a quick, beautiful fantasy of throwing her problems straight at the feet of the king, who could surely help her when no one else could....

But her father had something on him, too. Her father was the poison in everything.

You could try... something in her whispered.

Calista pulled away from her sister, then, and threw a couple more books into the satchel that already felt like a ton of bricks. And she tried very, very hard to keep her little surge of hope out of her voice. "All this royal nonsense is nothing but a distraction. It's not an avenue toward anything."

Melody sighed. "Once again, Calista. You will be the consort of the king. Any way you look at it, that's a more powerful position than vice president to a pig. If I were you, I would stop viewing the palace as an obstacle and start looking at it as an opportunity."

Calista couldn't believe that anyone could help her. But she had been willing to try— or think about trying—when the car the king had sent arrived to deliver her to the palace a few hours later.

"You remember what we're doing here," her father told her right before she left his house, pulling her aside as the palace staff loaded up the last of her things. He gripped her arm in that way she particularly didn't like, because it hurt. Though it had been years since she'd given him the satisfaction of wincing.

She didn't now, either.

"By *here*, I assume you mean the palace," she replied, not quite airily. "Not here as in right here in my childhood home."

It was a mark of how intense her father was

about all this that he didn't sneer or slap her. He only gripped her a little harder and moved her closer.

"It's your job to find something we can use against him, Calista," he growled at her, his face in hers. "Don't get your head turned by that fancy ring he gave you. That's window dressing and nothing more."

But she remembered Orion storming around that corner in the Skyros Media offices, as if he'd fully intended to charge her father and take him down. She remembered that look of dark fury on his royal face when he'd seen her father's handprint on her cheek. Maybe she really could ask him to help her. Maybe he was the only one who *could* help…

"What are you talking about?" she asked, no longer pretending to be the least bit *airy*. "I'm marrying him because you want me to. A total stranger, who I have nothing in common with, because he's the king. I thought that was what you wanted. I thought that was all you wanted."

"What I want is leverage over the palace," Aristotle told her harshly. "It was easy enough to find some on King Max. King Orion is harder—but we're not wasting prime positioning like this. You'll find something. You won't rest until you do. Do you understand me, girl? Because if you don't, it won't be you who suffers. I'll have your sister put away."

He had danced around that threat for years, but he'd never come out and said it like that before. So flat and matter-of-fact. So ugly and unmistakable.

Her head spun.

"You don't mean that," she said, though she knew better to argue.

"I will have her sanctioned and committed, girl," her father growled at her. "Her only use to me is the power it gives me over you, and believe me, I have every intention of using it. Test me, Calista. I dare you."

She thought her stomach might betray her, and swallowed, hard, to keep the panic down. To keep any further arguments to herself, because there was no point antagonizing him. There never was. But it was as if she couldn't help herself.

Because she couldn't allow anything to happen to Melody. But she just didn't see how she would do what her father wanted her to do. She didn't see how she could possibly find leverage on a man like Orion, so stalwart and *good*, damn him.

Of course he can't help you, she told herself. *No one can help you.*

Her father must have sensed a counterargument brewing, or worse, an appeal to the better nature he didn't have. He pinched her to stop it before it happened, hard enough to bring tears to her eyes. That was his farewell gift to the daughter he'd sold.

She had the whole ride over from her father's house to wait for the stinging to subside. And she had that little gift with her—bruising up nicely—when the palace staff ushered her, with no little pomp and circumstance, to the rooms she was told had been set aside for her use in the family wing.

"Quite an honor, madam, I don't mind saying," the stuffy butler had intoned down the length of his impressive nose.

Inside, alone, Calista had sat there in one of the sitting rooms. It was easily the most elegantly appointed room she'd ever beheld. And it made her feel lonelier than she ever had in her life.

She had no reason to imagine that would ever change.

Not when none of this was real, or hers. And when her brief was to gather incriminating information on the king while she was here so her father could continue to wield his repulsive influence. Or *thought* he could continue—until she took his company out from under him, which might be more difficult to pull off than she'd anticipated if she was locked up in the palace…

But her own self-pity was too much for her to bear. She wiped at her face, annoyed to find she'd actually let a few tears fall. She wandered through her suite until she found the bathroom and splashed water on her face until she felt a bit more like herself.

Feeling sufficiently pulled together, she went back out into the main hallway, and stopped. Because she came face-to-face with three officious-looking men.

"My goodness," she said mildly. "Have I already run afoul of the palace guard?"

"The palace guard would be armed, madam," said the one in the middle, with a bristling mustache. "We are His Majesty's private secretarial staff."

"Thank you," she murmured sweetly. "But I don't need any dictation at present."

And the three of them managed to look as if they might have swooned from horror, died from it and been resurrected, all without actually moving a muscle.

"We are here to see to your education, Lady Calista," intoned the mustache. "You will be married to His Majesty in only a matter of weeks. And unless I'm mistaken, you know very little indeed about palace life, royal etiquette, or any number of other things that will fall under your purview as queen and consort."

"Funnily enough," Calista said, glaring straight back at him, "the job was sold to me as a pretty simple one. Make an heir and go about my business. And as far as I'm aware, the making of heirs, even royal ones, doesn't involve a crowd."

But the mustache only smiled.

Pityingly.

And that was how, a week later, Calista

found herself actually looking forward to the first of the December holiday balls.

Her parents had practically had to throw her in the car and drag her to the palace before, but now she was already here in the palace. And she was so sick and tired of being followed around by the Trinity of Doom that she'd claimed she needed significantly more time to get ready than she actually did, and more, had actually taken that time. Because it turned out that the only thing better than a week at the spa—something she'd dreamed about but never done—was taking advantage of all palace life had to offer when it came to preparing for grand occasions.

A lovely, lengthy massage until the shoulders that were usually in her ears felt like butter. Her hair styled theatrically and her makeup applied just so. And a set of attendants to help her into a sumptuous gown that made her look like she belonged in a Disney movie.

It was almost enough to lull her into a false sense of security and well-being. It was almost enough to make her imagine this all might be real...

Almost.

She waited for Orion the way she always did, in that private salon of his that was now down the long hall instead of across town. She stood where she usually did, though it felt oddly intimate that she'd simply…walked here. Without a wrap, as she hadn't gone outside. She knew that the palace was a huge, sprawling complex, and yet the fact they now shared a roof seemed to lodge beneath her skin like its own pop of heat.

Don't be ridiculous, she chided herself.

But when Orion entered the room, at last, in all his kingly splendor, their eyes seemed to meet as if tugged together by magnetic forces. And then they held.

Calista told herself that she needed to hold on to her panic and fury about what was happening. That if she didn't, she would have no choice but to let go and lose herself in all that grave hazel.

"I'm told you're making progress," he said after the moment had long since turned awkward, and that made it easier.

"How patronizing." She scowled at him. "I

didn't realize that I was a remedial case. Or that progress reports were being issued."

But he didn't take the bait. He never took the bait.

"I feel certain that my secretaries impressed upon you that there was much you need to learn in a short period of time, Calista. And you cannot truly be surprised that they have let me know how the process has been unfolding, can you?"

That he sounded perfectly reasonable only made it worse. It made her want to hunker down and feed the fury in her whatever it needed to explode.

"I have learned many important things, Your Majesty."

Her voice was clipped and not exactly polite, and she decided on the spot that she would rather die than tell Orion that she'd enjoyed much of it. Not the endless corrections, but the scope of a queen's role—and all of it to be performed with grace and wit.

Assuming such attributes are at your disposal, the mustache had sniffed.

If she'd been planning to remain his queen, she might have found it a challenge in the best way to rise to the levels expected of the king's consort. The deft ability to influence ministers without appearing to do so. The political machinations hidden behind an easy smile. She would have loved getting to do those things—

But she wasn't going to be queen.

And she could be just as patronizing as he was. "I have heard a great many lectures on state dinners, for example. I have been informed that I must learn a certain fluency in the language of flowers, which is apparently very important, even though I have the blackest thumb imaginable. I have been forced to attempt every possible iteration of a curtsy, which should really be its own workout craze. *Royal Squats and Noble Lunges* has a nice ring to it, doesn't it? I have spent untold hours dissecting where, how, and to whom I may or may not incline my neck. All of this has been riveting." There was a gleam in his hazel eyes that made that fury inside her seem to melt. And caramelize. "Absolutely riveting."

"Yes, well. Not everything can be as exciting as prying into the personal lives of strangers with an eye to ripping their lives apart. It will no doubt be an adjustment."

Was it her imagination or was Orion rather more testy than usual tonight? Edgy, she might have said. If he was someone else.

"Is something the matter?" she asked, and it was only after she'd asked it that she realized she would have been better served pretending not to notice.

Because she certainly shouldn't care.

"Not at all," Orion said. "Or nothing more than usual. Sometimes it is not possible to rule a country. You must rule yourself and hope the country follows afterward. Eventually."

Calista had the urge to upend the nearest incidental table, scattering figurines and precious objects to and fro. She refrained. Barely.

She made herself breathe into the fury. "Self-control is admirable, I'm sure. Though I'm not certain it takes the place of, I don't know, basic human rights."

"Human rights?" He looked amazed then, and inarguably royal. As if he'd turned into a bust of himself. "Have human rights been violated in some fashion that I am unaware of, here on the quiet streets of Idylla?"

"Perhaps not on a wide scale. Not in Idylla, anyway." Admitting that felt like a surrender, and she didn't want to give up so much as a centimeter. "But I'm feeling rather concerned about my own rights at the moment."

"Yes." Orion eyed her. "I can see how you suffer."

"There's no need for sarcasm," she shot back at him. "You don't have the slightest idea what it's like to have your whole life taken away from you at a whim."

"Calista. I must beg of you." He shook his head. "Do you really think that I'm likely to lend a sympathetic ear to my blackmailer?"

"I'm not the one who blackmailed you."

"No, worse, you are my blackmailer's instrument."

There was something in his gaze, then. She didn't understand it. It was a glittering, dark sort of thing, and it made her skin prickle. Everywhere. It made that melting, caramelized mess she wanted to call fury...very distinctly something else, especially as it sank lower.

"Now you live beneath my roof. I receive

daily reports of the ways you challenge my staff. You treat me with rampant disrespect, so I am not particularly shocked that you are not the biddable girl they might wish you were. And none of it matters. I will marry you all the same, come Christmas Eve, because that is the tradition. You may not have been my choice, but you are my betrothed, and I do not break my promises." Orion's eyes gleamed, while his voice seemed to get tangled up in all that fire and fury within her. "But by all means, stand before me and tell me what it is like to have the life you'd planned snatched out of your fingers."

She blinked. Then again. "I suppose you have a point."

And to her surprise, he smiled. "You are the one who decided we must be enemies, Calista."

"Perhaps I was hasty."

Suddenly, it was as if she couldn't think what to do with her hands. Or her neck. She felt…outsized and awkward, and she knew, now, in no uncertain terms, that it would be inappropriate for her to sit until he did. That royal etiquette decreed that unless and until they sorted something else out for the two of them in private, she must continue to treat him with the courtesy due his station no matter how she felt about it.

The trouble isn't that you know, a voice in her whispered. *It's that you care.*

She rather thought she'd preferred it when she didn't.

"Did your parents get along?" she asked. He stared at her, and this time, there was no hoping she didn't flush. She did, and rather brightly, she feared. "I don't mean at the end. Everyone knows how...sad she became, of course. But surely they could not have begun at the place they ended." She swallowed, her throat suddenly dry. What had made her think bringing up the queen's death—officially called an accident but widely regarded as the suicide it was—was a good idea? No matter how the old queen was pitied because who *wouldn't* wish to escape from King Max? "Could they?"

Orion stalked over to the sideboard, and she watched as he fixed himself a drink with decisive, peremptory movements of his hands that made her feel a bit...fluttery.

He turned back, swirling liquid in a crystal tumbler, and eyed her rather darkly over the top of it.

"What is it exactly you are asking?"

"According to what I've learned in the past week, your mother was bred for the job," Calista said, still standing there feeling foolish with her hands folded in front of her and her back pin straight. Not because she felt in control, the way she did in a boardroom. But because she felt ripped into a million little pieces and she didn't have the slightest idea how to start putting them back together. So perfect posture it was. "She and your father were promised since the day of her birth. She was trained not only in how to be a queen, or how to be Queen of Idylla, for that matter, but how to be your father's specific queen. His likes and dislikes, his strengths and weaknesses. Other girls learned about history, but your mother? She studied your father."

"So I'm told, for her sins," Orion said darkly.

"Well? Did it work?"

Orion tossed back his drink. "To a point. Yes."

Calista wanted to fire questions at him, particularly because the look on his face then was troubled. But she bit her tongue. And though it was more difficult than it should have been to a seasoned negotiator, she waited.

Not at all sure he would reply until he did.

"While my grandfather was alive, it was different," he said. "My parents were newlyweds and from all I have ever been able to ascertain, they got along well enough. This was no love match, but then, no one expected it should have been. My mother was an excellent support for a crown prince. She provided the heir and the spare in short order. She maintained a full slate of complementary interests. She took great care to create a certain image—elegant, yet approachable. But then my grandfather died. My father became king."

"'Heavy is the head…'?"

"Heavy was the ego," Orion growled. "This is all documented history. It's not personal. My father was spectacularly ill suited to be the king of anything. He surrounded himself with the worst people. Sycophantic courtiers who told him only what he wished to hear.

He'd already secured the bloodline, so why not indulge himself as he pleased? He began to throw parties. He began to neglect his duties. And my mother, always trained to think first and only of my father, went with him wherever he led. How could she not?"

"She was a grown woman," Calista pointed out. Carefully. "A grown woman and a queen, in fact. With her own courtiers, advisers, and so on. Or so I am informed."

His mouth twisted. "If you already know, why are you asking me?"

"I want to know how you see this role I am to take in a few weeks." She lifted her chin and tried to understand why that severe look on his stark face made her want to do dangerous things. Like move closer. Or worse, touch him. "That's really what matters, isn't it? What do *you* want from a queen, Orion?"

She didn't understand why the tension in the room was so intense. But she also didn't move when he slapped his tumbler down on the sideboard with a decisive click, and then started for her.

Calista stood her ground. Somehow, she stood her ground, when he seemed to her like some kind of avenging angel as he bore down upon her.

And then his fingers were on her shoulders, pulling her close.

As if he wanted to flirt with the same dangers she did.

Because her secret shame was that there was not one single shred of resistance inside her. Not one, when she knew that this wasn't real. That none of this was anything but elaborate staging.

No matter how it felt.

"I've already told you what I want," he growled at her.

"Sex," she threw at him, because challenging him was the closest thing she had to a wall and she needed a wall. She needed *something* between them. "That's what you wanted from the start. You do know that you're the king, don't you? You can snap your fingers and have as much sex as you want with whoever you want. You don't have to marry unwilling women to get it."

She thought he ought to have been gripping her hard, as if he wanted to hurt her. The way her father would have done. But instead, his thumbs moved restlessly against the exposed skin of her clavicle. And she could feel the fire of it, the rhythm, the deep, drugging song as it spooled out inside her.

"I could snap my fingers, yes," he agreed, and if there was a wall between them it was made of need. "And then before I know it, I could also have a collection of tabloid articles to my name, one for each new scandal that would rip this kingdom apart. I prefer to keep my private life private. And all scandals in the past."

There was something in the way he said that. She tilted her head slightly to one side, trying to work it out. Something inside her longed to simply reach out her hand. To lay her palm against his cheek and feel the heat of him.

Another part of her wanted to bury her head against his chest, because she knew, somehow, that if she did, he would gather her against him and hold her tight.

But she could feel that song inside her, the pitch growing higher and more insistent.

And she thought of his mother, bred since her birth to play the supporting role. To disappear while standing in plain sight, there next to her husband. A woman created for the sole purpose of bearing children and smiling prettily beneath the weight of a crown that was never hers.

Calista understood something terrible about herself then. She understood exactly how she'd been lying to herself all this time.

She'd worked so hard, and sacrificed everything, but not only because she wanted to save her sister from her parents. Not only because she wanted to put her father in his place at last.

She'd been doing it for those reasons, yes. But more than that, she'd wanted her own power. She'd wanted to prove that she *could* do it. She alone. She'd wanted the life she knew she could have had if she'd been born the son her father had always wanted.

She had never trusted anyone.

She didn't see herself starting now.

And it had all happened too quickly, hadn't it? She'd been removed from Skyros Media. She'd been shunted off to the palace. She'd spent a week learning about all the ways she could better serve and support the king.

Calista didn't know if it was galling or pathetic that she'd already drowned, had disappeared in her own mirror, and was the last to know.

"I've already said this to you once," she said now, swaying closer to him because it felt like danger, and that felt like resistance. "You don't have to go to all these lengths to have sex with me, Your Majesty. You could do it right now, if you wanted. All you have to do is ask."

"We have a ball to get to," he gritted out at her, but his thumbs brushed against her skin. And he didn't let her go.

"My bad," she replied, smiling because that felt meaner. Edgier and therefore safer. "I should have known. You only want me if it's a challenge. If there's some kind of hunt. Even kings are mere men, after all."

"Hardly," Orion growled. "I just want you, damn you."

And then he slammed his mouth to hers.

CHAPTER SEVEN

ORION SHOULDN'T HAVE let her goad him. He should have been better than that.

More controlled. More in command of himself—and her.

But as Calista's taste exploded in his mouth—far better than he remembered, far darker and wilder and more addictive—he found he didn't much care.

He wasn't the fool she thought he was.

Orion knew that she was acting out. That despite her performance that first day, she was in many ways a victim of her father the same as he was.

He knew all that. He simply couldn't care about it the way he ought to have. Not just then.

Because she tasted like all the dreams he'd been having, one hotter than the last. Intense and demanding and astonishingly perfect.

She was every fire he'd ever known and denied himself, burning hot within him. Making him think she was something he could not possibly survive intact—

But immolation sounded good to him just then. And tasted better.

He knew that they had a schedule to keep. He knew that their car was waiting to take them to the ball, and more important, all the people who had bought tickets would be waiting for them, too. He knew that this particular holiday tradition, with or without a royal engagement in the mix, was beloved by his people. They looked forward to it all year, and it was part of their national character to note, with pride, that Idylla boasted a season for commoners and kings to dance and make merry together.

His father had started blowing off the holiday balls years ago, to no one's great surprise. But Orion never had. In fact, as crown prince, he'd never missed one.

Orion was always where he said he would be. He was always on time and prepared. If his schedule decreed that he would set foot on a certain flagstone at 6:37 p.m., that was precisely when his foot struck the earth.

"It's easy to be a monk when you rid your life of any temptation," Griffin had told him, years ago.

Orion had ignored him back then. He'd assumed that was no more than Griffin being provocative, as ever.

But tonight, Calista was in his arms, her mouth was open beneath his as she kissed him back, and Orion understood at last that he had never been tested before.

He had never come close to a test.

That should have appalled him, but it didn't. It couldn't. Because he was kissing her, and that was all he could manage to care about.

He kissed her like a dying man. He kissed her as if she alone could quench the great thirst he hadn't known he had. He kissed her and he kissed her, moving closer and pulling her even tighter in against him. He angled his head, kissing her hungrily. Hotly.

He wanted to sink his hands into her hair. He wanted to throw her down on the nearest flat surface and truly indulge himself at last.

He *wanted*.

And that meant he was as weak as his father had ever been.

It was that thought that penetrated, dousing him like sheets of ice.

He thrust her away from him, taking in the fact that she looked as wrecked he was. That her eyes were glassy, her mouth soft.

But he couldn't process any of that.

All he could think was that after all this, after everything he'd done, after the years and years of keeping himself separate from the things that tempted other men because he wanted to be something better, something more, something worthy of the crown he now wore—in the end, it all came down to this.

Petty sins of the flesh.

A lifetime of control and commitment and all it took was one woman to ruin him. He almost laughed, though nothing was funny.

"Is this why your father sent you here?" His voice was rough and thick, two signs that he was already too far gone. "Is this the game you're playing? Just like every other honey trap that has ever been set for me?"

For a moment, she seemed to vibrate. Her aquamarine eyes were wide and glued to his, but the look in them was haunting.

Because it was the same one he'd seen on

her face in that hallway in Skyros Media. Right after her father had literally slapped her cheek.

Orion had now done the same himself, with his mouth.

Did he really need any further evidence that at the slightest provocation, at the first temptation, he became his father?

He remembered his mother, then, though he preferred not to think of her outside of a few stray, happy memories when he was small. But now he remembered those later years. How she would cry and wail, literally crumbling if King Max so much as glanced in her direction. Cringing and sobbing, until Griffin and Orion, though only boys themselves, had been forced to act as her protectors.

Deep down, Orion's secret shame was that he'd grown impatient with her. His own mother.

You can't cry in front of him, he'd told her once, furiously, with all the conviction of the overly serious child he'd been. *You can't show him that he's hurt you.*

But she had only done it more.

This time, he assured himself, he would do

no such thing, no matter the provocation tonight. It surely wasn't *her* fault that he was so tempted by her. He waited for Calista to cringe away from him, assuring himself that he would understand her. He would support her. He would do whatever was necessary to—

But instead, she laughed.

It was scornful, bracing laughter, as much a relief as it was an assault.

Her hands found her hips, and she scowled at him, and all of that was better than cringing, certainly. Though Orion couldn't say that it was *comfortable*, exactly. Or that he liked it much. Only that it was better than the alternative.

"Honey trap," she repeated, as if he'd called her a filthy name. "You must be joking."

"Your father could have used the leverage he had on my father to do any number of things," Orion said, perhaps a bit gruffly. "He chose to force our marriage. You tell me why a honey trap isn't the first thing that would come to mind under the circumstances."

"First I'll point out the distinct lack of honey in the trap," she retorted, her voice arch. "Who knew that the King of Idylla himself could be lured in with this much vinegar? I don't really know what that says about you, Orion. But I don't think it's good."

He wanted to kiss her again. He wanted to peel her out of those clothes and keep his mouth on her until she melted against him. And then he wanted to taste every last inch of her skin, until both of them were immolated. Until there was no telling the difference between spark and flame, fire and heat.

Him and her.

He was so hard it hurt.

But the hurt was a good thing. It was like a hair shirt, to carry on with his brother's favorite monk analogy. It reminded him who he was.

"We have a ball to attend," he told her, taking a deep pleasure in the fact he could sound so mild. So unbothered. He could see temper flash over her, and enjoyed that even more. "I don't say this to stop you taunting me. Carry on all you like. You'll just need to do it in the car."

When he beckoned for her to precede him out of the room, he thought she might balk.

He waited, oddly primed and charged, as she stared back at him, her hands in markedly unladylike fists at her sides.

Inside, he *wanted*. He ached with it.

And what was the matter with him that there was a very large part of him that wanted nothing more than for her to launch herself in his direction? For her to take a swing at him, even—the way no one else would dare?

Because one way or another, that would allow him to put his hands on her?

Instead, Calista lifted her chin, gathered the skirts of her dress in those fists of hers, and swept out of the room.

And he was a little too aware of the tension between them as they sat in the car, building up their defenses again, brick by brick. He consulted his mobile. He took calls that could have waited, had he wanted them to wait. All the while, Calista pointedly repaired her makeup and hair. He wondered if she knew how it felt to him—like she was easing those iron bars between them back into place. And locking them up, separately, in their original prisons.

He told himself he ought to have been grateful.

Tonight's event was at the Royal Botanical Gardens, with portable heaters everywhere to ward off what passed for the chill in this first week of December. The gardens were lit up, with little lights sprinkled everywhere, so that more than one person remarked that it was as if they'd been set down in their very own Christmas ball. The sort that one could hang on a tree, and build traditions around—

Not that Orion, raised as he was by wolves in royal form, had ever had anything of the kind. Trees festooned about the palace, bristling with decorations, certainly. But their only family traditions involved making themselves scarce while King Max raged, then collapsed in a drunken stupor.

He spent a long while circulating through the crowd, doing his best to mimic the sort of man who was filled with Christmas cheer.

Still, when the first waltz started, he knew his duty as king and therefore, always, the guest of honor. He wanted to touch Calista just then about as much as he wanted to punch himself in the face, but he swept her into his arms anyway, because it was expected.

And for a few moments, they danced in pointed silence.

But only for a few moments.

"This is really taking your martyr act a step too far," she said when she could clearly take the quiet no longer, though she smiled joyfully up at him while she said it.

"I don't know what you mean."

"You do." Her smile widened. "It really is so boring, Orion. It's one thing to crucify yourself on every stray piece of wood that crosses your path in the palace. But it's something else again, I think, to fling yourself upon the altar of your own self-importance *in public.*"

He took his time looking down at her, and if he held her a shade too close, well. The crowds would have to deal with it. He was the bloody king.

"I will repeat. I don't know what you mean."

The spark of challenge lit up those eyes of hers, and suddenly, he could think of nothing but her fists at her side in that private parlor.

And how surprised he'd been that she didn't swing then.

He should have known that, of course, she'd waited.

"Don't you?" she asked, still looking—to someone not quite as close to her as he was—happy and filled with appropriate seasonal delight. "I thought you prided yourself on being such a rational man. Such a reasonable king after all our dark years with your father." She made a tutting sound. "How tragic not to know yourself at all."

"Perhaps a better conversation would be to investigate what it is you know about yourself, Calista," he replied, and it was like a song inside him, almost as good as his mouth on hers. "As far as I can tell, you've made yourself your father's handmaid. You prance around in your corporate costume. You shout at anyone who will listen about your importance. But at the end of the day, the first moment he could sell you, he did. Even pawns are treated better than that, surely."

"You are the reigning expert on pawns, of course," she replied coolly.

"Whose pawn am I?"

"My father's, for one thing." She smirked at him. "Look at that. We have something in common after all."

He thought it wise, then, to finish off the dance with less talking. Because for the first time in his life, in as long as he could remember, he wasn't entirely certain that he remained as in control of himself as he ought to have been.

And he wasn't even kissing her.

That notion was so astounding—so hideous, really—that when the waltz ended he executed a stark, stiff sort of bow, and stalked away from her.

Better to leave his fiancée on the dance floor abruptly than to descend into…whatever it was that moved in him, dark and dangerous, that had everything to do with the taste of her, still there on his tongue.

Far more potent than wine or spirits.

The night wore on. Nobility and dignitaries danced attendance on him, as ever. He posed for a thousand pictures, trying to exude calm. Quiet certainty. As if his very presence was a happy ending. One the whole country had been waiting for, all this time.

Not that he knew much about such things. Still, he tried.

Toward the end of the night, conscious that it was impolite for anyone to leave until he did, Orion once again sought out Calista. The gardens looked mysterious at night. All the sparkling lights and the glow from the heaters gave the winding paths an almost unearthly glow. Orion walked with no apparent haste, as if he was out for a stroll, enjoying that even he could find a measure of anonymity in the shadows. And when he was seen, he gave no indication that he was looking for a woman who, had she been anyone else, would have been stuck to his side all night to advance her position.

There was a part of him that liked her more than he should because she was nothing like the sort of socialite heiress he'd always assumed he would marry, all soft smiles to the face and a dulcet-toned knife to the back. Calista, he knew, would come at him from the front.

Something about that was deeply cheering.

He rounded a corner festooned with exultant shrubberies, then, and saw her. At last.

The soft light surrounded her, making her glow as if she was her own candle, and Orion felt...poleaxed. Frozen solid, there where he stood, though the Mediterranean night was nowhere near freezing.

As if he'd never seen a woman before.

His heart exploded inside his chest, so dramatic a sensation that he was half-afraid he'd suffered the kind of cardiac arrest that had claimed his father. But no, he realized after a breath, he was still standing.

It took him long moments—small eternities, really—to realize first, that Calista wasn't alone. She stood with her father, here in a far-off corner of the gardens. Though she was still dressed like a queen—*his* queen—she had her arms crossed and a faint frown marring her perfect brow.

Unless he was very much mistaken, her father was threatening her. He recognized that particular bulldog-like expression on Skyros's face.

"Whatever it takes, girl," Aristotle said to her, sounding angry. "You understand me?"

"Perfectly," Calista replied, her voice cool and crisp.

Orion should have stayed there, half concealed in shadow, to see what would happen next. He knew he should. But Aristotle reached out, as if to grip Calista's arm, and he couldn't stand it.

He couldn't *allow* it.

"Careful there, Skyros," he found himself belting out into the dark. "I believe we already covered this."

Father and daughter jerked, then turned to gape at him. And he couldn't say he cared that Calista looked faintly guilty, because what really mattered to him was that Aristotle dropped his hand.

"You do have a habit of popping up in the strangest places, don't you?" Aristotle growled.

Orion ignored him, inclining his head toward Calista. "The hour grows late, my lady. It's time to head back to the palace."

"Indeed," she said, shooting a look at her father that Orion wasn't sure he wanted to be able to read. "I wouldn't want to turn into a pumpkin."

Orion held out his hand. And he didn't know if she was performing for her father. He didn't know far too many things when it came to this woman he was meant to marry, it was true. But he couldn't worry about any of that as he should, because she stepped toward him and took his hand then, and for a moment, he almost thought she meant it.

For a moment, he was tempted to forget that he hadn't chosen her himself.

He nodded at her father, his tormentor, and then swept her away so that she could join him in the endless ordeal of extricating himself from the ball.

By the time they made it to the car, he'd grown so used to her hand in his that he felt a flash of something like grief, though far hotter, when she took it away.

And this time, though they both sat in the back of the car just as they had on the way to the ball, it was different. It was as if the same heartbeat pounded through both of them. Orion was aware of the blood rushing through him. He was aware of Calista, as if she was wrapped tight around him. As if she was goading him directly, when all she was doing was sitting there beside him, staring straight ahead.

He was aware of her breath, the rise and fall of her chest. And of the faint scent of the perfume she favored, light enough and seductive enough that he was never quite sure if he was imagining it.

Once in the palace they walked side by side, their footsteps echoing against the marble floors as they headed, together, for the family wing.

"I will escort you to your suite," he informed her, aware that his voice was gravelly. Low. Unduly serious.

And not quite his own.

"What's this?" Her voice was bright, if forced. Tense, the same as his. "Are we suddenly observing dating protocols? However will my tender heart cope?"

He walked next to her, that throbbing, pounding beat inside him still insistent. Dark and stirring. And it only got worse with every step.

"I will not ask you why you are forever hiding away in dark corners, whispering with your father, a man already known to the crown as a bad actor. A legitimate threat."

"I'm glad you won't ask. Because I wouldn't answer you anyway. He's my father."

"Nor will I ask you what it is he wants you to do, as I think we both know you wouldn't tell me anyway."

"That would defeat the purpose, surely, having gone to all the trouble to slip a king into a pocket in the first place."

Her voice was tart, but somehow, he thought that darkness in her gaze was the real truth. Or maybe it was only that he felt the same darkness in him.

"But it does beg the question, Calista," he said, as they drew up outside the door to her suite. "Which one of us is the greater martyr?"

She flinched at that, as if the question was another slap. And he watched, amazed—and something far darker than merely *amazed*—as her cheeks flushed red.

"I'm the very opposite of a martyr, thank you."

"Not from where I'm standing. Don't you have a sister? Where is she in all this?"

Calista surged forward, her aquamarine eyes clouded with some great emotion. And then, to his eternal astonishment, thumped him.

In the chest.

Hard.

"Don't you mention my sister. Don't you try to drag her into this. She has her own troubles, and certainly doesn't need palace drama on top of it."

"Are you sure?" Orion asked with an idleness he did not feel. "Are you protecting your sister because she needs protection? Or because you like how it feels to be the one forever in demand? The one forever spreading out the mantle of your many sacrifices far and wide, so you can complain about them?"

She thumped him again, and it was clarifying.

Because it was rage inducing. Though, if he thought about it, it wasn't rage at all that surged in him then.

It was hot, dark and deep, but it wasn't quite *rage*.

And the truth was, he felt that hair shirt disintegrating all around him. He could hardly remember the vows he'd made, or why.

Because even though she was thumping him, which would have bordered on a treasonous assault if anyone else had done it, all he could seem to focus on was that she was touching him.

Calista was *touching him*, and of her own volition.

That felt far stronger than any vow.

"You haven't the slightest idea what it's like," she threw at him.

"Says a civilian to a king."

Temper flashed over her face, and there was something almost electric about it. He could feel the same currents from earlier, but they were hotter now. Brighter.

As if the two of them, together, burned like a fever.

And she appeared to be just getting started. "You don't know the first thing about real life. You don't know about loss. You don't know what it's like to work your whole life for something only to have it snatched away from you at the last second."

"I am being blackmailed into marrying you, Calista, though I am the bloody king— and not my father. Perhaps it is you who do not understand."

"I have fought my whole life," she seethed at him. "Any sacrifices I made were not to martyr myself so I could feel better about my choices, but because they were necessary. Life and death, Orion. You weren't the only one who grew up under the whims of a terrible father. And not everyone gets to be a crown prince in that scenario. Some of us have to suffer in private. But you wouldn't know anything about that, because you live in a gilded palace, making laws and issuing commandments. You should try the real world sometime."

"Lady Calista. Please. You are the daughter of a billionaire. You live in an island kingdom the poets call enchanted. Magical. A real-life fairy tale. Perhaps you are no more acquainted with the real world than I."

She blew out a breath at that, as if she was deflating there before his eyes. And he had the impression she wasn't entirely aware of it when instead of thumping him again, her hand flattened out, so that her palm was resting in the hollow between his pectoral muscles.

Calista might not be aware of it, but he could think of nothing else.

And for a moment, their gazes remained tangled together, and they…breathed.

As if they shared that same breath.

"I wish…" she began. "I wish that I could… You and I…"

But she didn't finish.

Orion reached up and covered her hand with his, trapping her there against his chest.

And he couldn't tell if that was her heartbeat he felt, or his own. Only that it rang in him like a warning. Like a new song.

"Then do something about it," he told her.

A command. A plea. His own *want*.

He should have known better. He should never have risked it. The control he never, ever lost felt loose around him then, precarious and dangerously close to breaking.

Orion needed to take his leave of her. He needed to pretend none of tonight had happened. He needed to march off, regain his equilibrium, and remind himself who he was, and more, who he wanted to be.

But he didn't move.

Not when she smiled, a curve of her lips that was not smirky, or edgy, or any of the weapons it usually was.

And certainly not when Calista lifted herself up onto her toes, swayed in closer, and finally kissed him.

Setting them both alight.

CHAPTER EIGHT

CALISTA FELT TWISTED. Turned inside out, and raw straight through.

But kissing Orion was a revelation.

Because it didn't make her feel less twisted, less raw or inside out. It took all of that and made it all worse, and then, by some delirious magic that only he seemed to know, heated it all up and made it better.

Until all she wanted was more.

She kissed him, her hand against his chest and his hand on hers, and he followed her lead. And it felt the way she'd always imagined fairy tales would, in those stories that belonged to others.

Soft. Sweet.

The faintest hint of heat and need—

But then Orion shifted, angled his jaw, and everything...*ignited*.

He kissed her and he kissed her.

And she forgot her goals here. She forgot

all the bold words she'd thrown at him when they'd met, or the promises she'd made herself about how this would go down. She forgot everything, because he tasted too good.

Because nothing about this situation was real…but he was.

This was.

She let out a soft sound as she felt the hard wall behind her, but then the harder, far more fascinating wall of his body was pressed up against the front of her, and that was delicious. And everywhere. And she'd had no idea she could burn like this, so hot and bright.

She wound her arms around his neck and lost herself in the dance of their tongues, the taste of him, and a lifetime or two could have passed that way. Maybe they did.

But the heat was growing. The need wound around and around inside her, coiling tight, then tighter still, until she worried she might crack open. And when Orion lifted her against him so she could wrap her legs around his waist, she could do nothing but groan out her approval.

His kisses were deep, wild, perfect. But

there was too much in the way. Her dress with its voluminous skirts seemed to anticipate her growing need and counter it, and all the clothes he wore seemed like an affront.

And it was as if he read her mind, because he pulled back, then. He tore his mouth from hers, but didn't put her down. For a moment all she could do was pant and wonder if her heart could really beat that hard without hurting her, and then Orion was shouldering his way into her suite, holding her against him as easily as if she weighed no more than a handful of feathers.

There was something about it. Something about being *carted about* by a man. *Effortlessly.* It made her feel feminine and sweet in all the ways she'd never been, like spun sugar. A confection.

The kind of dessert she couldn't wait for him to sample.

He carried her straight through to the bedroom without breaking his stride, then set her down at the foot of the grand bed that stood gracefully against the far wall. Across from it, the fire had been lit and danced there in its stone hearth, sending light and shadow spinning into the elegant room.

In the flickering of the flames, Orion's face seemed carved from marble, taut with need, and marked with a passion so intense it made his hazel eyes dark.

And better still, made her shudder, deep within. Where she felt exactly the way he looked.

"Orion..." she whispered, though she didn't know what she meant to say. Or how she could say it when she was so wild with wanting him, it hurt.

"I want you," he said, as if he knew. And his voice was thick with it.

With something else, too, though she couldn't place it.

It was not until his hands found her face to slide along her cheeks, then his fingers dug into her hair and pulled it loose from its pins, that she realized what it was.

Wonder.

The word seemed to shimmer inside her, heat and flame. But then he was kissing her again, and everything became a part of that.

The slide of his tongue. The dizzying, glorious mastery he took of her.

And then when he pulled back and gazed at her as if he'd never beheld such beauty.

Calista felt lit up from the inside out, and trembled with it, especially when all Orion did was smile.

A very male, very dark sort of smile.

And then he undressed her.

But he didn't simply rip her clothes off, or hurry them along in any way.

He…unwrapped her, as if every bit of flesh he uncovered was a gift and he had nothing better to do than savor it. For eternity, if necessary.

Because that was what he did. He took his time, lavishing attention as much on the space between her breasts as the aching crest of each. He learned her collarbone, her shoulders, and each of her fingers. He spent a lifetime on the line of her spine, the curve of her lower back, the flare of her hips. Calista lost days, weeks, months, as he found his way down the length of each leg, then up again.

And by the time he made it between, to that place where she ached for him the most—

molten and sweet and hot—she was gasping for breath.

Then her gasps turned to cries as he tasted her there, too.

Orion feasted on her with a fierce, possessive intensity that had her first falling back against the foot of the bed, and then lifting her hips up to meet the flat of his tongue, the faint scrape of his teeth, right where she needed it most.

And the first time she broke apart, arching up against him and sobbing, she understood fully why the French called it a little death.

Though there was nothing *little* about it.

Orion shifted her, moving her farther back onto the bed. Calista simply…lay there, fighting for air, as he rid himself of the suit he wore at last.

And then, despite how hard it still was to breathe, she had to prop herself up on her elbows to watch. Because the truth about the King of Idylla was that he was far more beautiful naked than he was magnificently clothed. He was a work of art. He belonged on all the statues that cluttered up this palace, and she was half-afraid that her heart would clatter its way straight out of her chest, because she was going to get to touch him. All of him.

She was going to get to lose herself in all that spectacular maleness, and even imagining that made her flush. Everywhere.

And the look on his face as he regarded her, sprawled out naked on the bed while she waited for him, almost made her tip straight over that edge again.

It was so intense. *Too* intense, almost. He looked at her with so much focused ferocity that she felt fluttery.

And then he crawled his way up onto the bed to join her, and that only made the intensity and the fluttering worse.

Better, something in her argued.

"I want to touch you," she whispered. "I want to taste you."

"Next time," he growled.

Calista meant to protest, but he was kissing her again. Deep, drugging, intense kisses that sent her spinning.

And when Orion finally gathered her in his arms, then rolled her beneath him, she could feel how close to out of control he was. She could feel that electric tremor in him, running through him, as if he'd plugged himself into a wall socket.

His kisses grew wilder. More glorious.

And then she could feel him, the hardest part of him, flush up against the place where she wanted him the most.

It was almost too much to handle.

He blew out a breath, and she could feel his heart pounding against hers. His gaze was dark, gleaming with a kind of fierce longing, and she could hardly bear the intensity of this moment.

She could hardly bear this.

Him.

She felt as if they were both caught in a mad storm. It howled and shook the windows, but in the center of everything was Orion. In the way he notched himself into her soft heat, and then waited there, one heartbeat. Another.

And she thought there could be nothing in the world more real, more true, than this. No matter how they'd gotten here. No matter what their future held. Wanting him made her feel open wide and utterly bared, and the craziest part was that she longed for that, too.

For someone to look at her the way he did, as if he'd never wanted anything more and never, ever would.

"Please," Calista whispered. "*Please*, Orion."

And with a deep kind of growl, he thrust forward and buried himself within her.

Calista fell apart. She burst into a thousand pieces, when she would have said it was impossible for her to have hit such heights again at all tonight. Much less so soon.

She shook and she shook. And when the glorious quaking subsided, she was still clutching him to her.

But he hadn't moved.

"Orion…" she whispered.

There was a grimness about that stark expression on his face as he braced himself above her. As if he was holding himself so tightly that the slightest movement might break him.

And suddenly Calista wanted nothing more than to see him break. To see the reserved, guarded king break apart the way she had. So she shifted, rolling her hips to take him even deeper into her, and he let out a sound that could have been a laugh.

Though perhaps it sounded a bit more tortured.

But then, finally, he began to move.

And the storm they'd made moved in, wrapped itself around them, and began to howl.

Or maybe that was Calista. She couldn't tell.

Orion set a rhythm, but she didn't want that. She didn't want patience when she'd already lost hers so completely. She didn't want a single second more of his regal composure.

So she wrapped her legs around his waist and set her teeth to his neck. She met each thrust. And she knew the exact moment when King Orion Augustus Pax, King of Idylla, simply…lost it.

He dropped his head to her shoulder. His hips pistoned, tossing her straight back into that wildfire she'd thought had already burned its way out of her. Twice.

But it turned out there was so much more to burn.

He hurtled them both over that cliff, and his

mouth against her shoulder while he went. And somewhere between those two things—the way he lost himself and the way he found himself with his mouth against her flesh—took her with him.

Tossing them over the edge and into oblivion.

Together.

She had no sense of falling asleep, though she knew she must have when she woke to find herself lifted up in Orion's arms. A faint alarm stirred deep inside her, but she ignored it, because perhaps not every last second of her life had to be a fight. A struggle.

It was far better to rest her head on his shoulder the way she imagined regular women might, and dream a bit as he carried her through the suite, and deposited her into the huge bathtub already full and foaming.

Calista slid into the embrace of the water, smiling, because she couldn't remember the last time someone had cared for her. That was her job. And she smiled wider when he surprised her completely and joined her.

Then liked it even more when he shifted

her around so he could hold her, her back to his front.

And held like that, where no one could see her, the hot water could sink into her bones, and Calista could simply…be.

It felt like a revolution.

She let herself relax, as if nothing outside the confines of this tub could touch her. Or could matter, one way or the other. No schemes, no goals, no worries. Just the warm water, the bubbles, and Orion.

Calista rested against him, and let the quiet soothe her. Or maybe it was him, so solid and strong behind her.

She sighed a little when he picked her hand out of the water and held it between them, once again fiddling with the ring he'd put there. The Ring of Queens. The ring, it was rumored, a besotted ruler of Idylla had created for his beloved, fashioning it from sky and sea, so she could wear it forever on her finger and think of Idylla. Of him.

And for the first time since this farce had started, Calista found herself really imagining what it would be like if this was real. If the only thing she had to do was become Orion's queen. If all the rest of it was a skin she could shed when they married, and once they did she could simply be the sort of woman who could wear a ring like this all the time, without irony. She could be the kind of woman he could hold in his arms the way he did now, the whole rest of the world at bay.

The kind of woman who could allow herself to be as real as he felt to her.

All she had to do was imagine herself anyone else alive, and this moment would have been romantic. A beautiful new beginning. The start of an unexpected chapter in the kind of arranged marriages families like hers had been mandating forever.

But wishes were never horses, and Calista didn't get to play Cinderella games. She didn't have a fairy godmother. Instead, she had a nasty, terrible father… And what was she doing?

The water was still warm, but she felt cold. How could she let herself sit here, surrendering to all these treacherous feelings for this man when nothing could ever come of them?

This could never be real. This was only a game, and if it was a game, that meant she had to win it. She couldn't let either one of them be lulled into any false senses of security when there was none.

Not when so much was at stake. Not when Melody would be the one to pay the price.

Every wish, every feeling inside her was a betrayal of her sister. Calista should have hated herself.

She squeezed her eyes shut, happy that he couldn't see her face or the torment there that shouldn't have been there, and made herself laugh. A sharp dagger of a laugh, precisely calculated to make him stiffen beneath her.

Which he did, and her heart ached. But she kept going.

Because he was her adversary, not her lover, and she really didn't know how she'd let herself forget that for a moment.

"I really am shocked, Orion," she said, making her voice arch. Insinuating. A hideous intrusion into the beauty of this moment, and she hated herself for it. But she didn't stop. "How on earth have you managed to keep your lovers from prattling on to all the tabloids about your prowess in bed? I would have thought they'd be lining up to talk about how good you are. To compare notes, even, the better to brag to each other and all the poor women out there who can only dream of touching you."

Calista wanted to cry. She couldn't let herself, however, so instead she laughed again. Another sharp knife.

And she could feel him change beneath her, going stern and harsh.

You did that, she snarled at herself. *Good job.*

It wasn't lost on her that she should have been happy that she'd done it.

"I'm not a show pony, Calista." His voice was disapproving and dark. And she could feel it inside her as if every word was carved into her ribs. Flaying her open, and deservedly. "I do not perform for the crowds—much less the filthy tabloids."

"You don't have to perform. You're you." That almost veered back into the mess of feelings that made her throat feel tight, so she kept on with that bright, brittle blade of a laugh. "And you must be some kind of magical creature to keep them all so quiet all these years. I'm not sure it's ever happened before in the history of royalty."

"I do not care to share my private life," he said, his voice a rumbling bit of thunder that she could feel against her back like a new, worse storm. "I have been at some pains to tell you this."

"Not everyone gets to choose what they keep private, Orion. Especially not when they sit on thrones and expect others to bow and scrape before them. I'm amazed you haven't learned that lesson already."

"Perhaps you will need to teach it to me," he said then, a different, silky note in his voice. It made her shudder, and she wasn't sure if that was pure sensual reaction or some kind of foreboding. "Because there is only one person who can talk to the tabloids or anyone else about my sexual prowess, Calista. I have not had to use magic spells to ensure any particular loyalty from anyone. I've maintained a dignified silence about my exploits by simply…not having any."

She didn't understand.

She blinked at the tub and the water before

her. "Is that a fancy way of saying you made them all sign nondisclosure agreements?"

But he didn't reply. He simply stayed where he was, lounging there in the hot bath behind her, his back like a wall. And she turned the word she'd said over and over again in her head.

And then again, when an inkling bloomed inside her.

"Orion."

He sounded amused. "Calista."

"You don't… You can't mean…?"

"Indeed I do."

Calista pushed away from him. Something great and terrible was expanding inside her chest, fast and hot. And she really didn't know if it was a sob or if she was about to scream, or some mad combination of both—

"You can't…?"

She turned around in the water, ignoring the way it sloshed alarmingly at the sides of the tub. Then she knelt there, facing him.

Her heart kicking at her so hard she was astonished she wasn't running flat out.

His eyes glittered dark gold. But otherwise, he looked almost entirely at his ease. His mouth in its usual stern line. His head high. Not in the least bit concerned about what he'd just told her.

What he'd just admitted to her.

"You can't possibly mean…?" she whispered.

"That is exactly what I mean," he replied, quietly. Almost as if he was relishing this, she thought. "You are my only lover, Calista. And soon to be my wife and queen. Your reaction suggests you did not enjoy yourself when I feel certain you did."

"I… That's not the point! You're supposed to disclose things like that!"

He lifted a shoulder, then lowered it, looking entirely unconcerned. "I apologize if this upsets you in some way."

"Upsets me?" She felt a deep, shuddering thing, rattling through her. As if her bones were coming apart. *As if your heart is breaking,* something in her whispered. "Of course it doesn't upset me, I just don't believe it."

She didn't know what she imagined a virgin ought to look like—or someone who had so recently been a virgin—but she was sure it wasn't this. Orion, every inch of him majestic in all ways, lounging back in the bath they shared. An enigmatic look on his face and not a single shred of anything like insecurity about his performance or her reaction anywhere.

Not that he should have been insecure. But surely there should have been fumbling. Mistakes or even misfires. Not…all that fierce possession that made her clench with need all over again, just thinking of it.

"Why would a man lie about such a thing?" he asked idly. "Surely it is more likely that the lies go in the other direction. Men do like to spin tales of their prowess, do they not?"

The gleam in his dark gaze suggested that he knew full well that he did not need to brag about his prowess or anything else. That, too, made a shiver snake its way down her spine.

"But you… But that…" She ordered herself to stop stammering. To get a hold of herself. "How?"

There was the faintest curve in the corner of Orion's mouth, then. He kept his dark gold gaze on her. "It was clear to me from a very young age that one of the primary ways in which my father was weak was his complete inability to avoid the sexual invitations that came his way. He did nothing to hide them. Indeed, he flaunted his various conquests in magazines like your father's or right here in the palace. And at the age when I might have started experimenting with such things, I was too busy engaged in what was already my life's work. Cleaning up his messes." His eyes glittered. "I decided I had no need to clean up mine, as well. It started as a rash decision when I was no more than thirteen. But it became a vow, and I kept it."

"How did you possibly…?"

Calista couldn't finish the sentence. She was terribly afraid that her heart was going to claw its way out of her chest, right there in the tub. She felt weak, somehow. And more profoundly thrown than she ever had before.

Or maybe, a voice inside her that sounded suspiciously like her sister whispered, *what you actually feel is vulnerable.*

Because he had given her something he had kept to himself all this time. He had made this thing between them real, and it made her want to sob. She wanted to lean forward, take his hands in hers, or his face, and tell him to be careful. That she could not be trusted and would only betray him in the end. How could he not know that already?

"Do you imagine that men cannot control themselves?" Orion sounded amused again. "I will note that no one thinks anything of it if a woman chooses to hold on to her virtue. But there must be something wrong with a man if he does the same."

"You did this to stay virtuous?"

"My brother would tell you that I'm ill-suited to be a king, because the monastic life suits me so much better." Again, the hint of a smile played with his mouth. Not as if he couldn't understand her reaction. But as if he found it entertaining. "I have always been intensely physical. I have merely restricted myself to other expressions of it. Until now." He inclined his head. "Until you."

That same emotion walloped her again. Was she going to surrender to it and sob? Or was she going to let it wrench her apart? Was she mad to imagine she could choose when it felt as if she might burst where she sat?

"All that waiting and you just thought, *Enough's enough*, after a night at a ball."

"With the woman I am to marry," Orion said, with tremendous patience and another hint of laughter. "When if not now? It wasn't marriage I was saving myself for, Calista. I'm not a young girl with a hope chest. I simply wished to make certain that I would not repeat my father's mistakes."

"But—"

He moved then, hooking his hand around her neck and tugging her gently to him, so she fell against his chest. And the curse of it was, she liked it there. She fit him too well, and she had to close her eyes against the surge of unfortunate sensation that stirred up in her.

"This is an arranged marriage," she said crossly. "This is supposed to be distant and remote and chilly. Not...*this*."

"I think we'll muddle through, Calista. Somehow."

There was something about the way he said her name, then. It had changed. Or she had changed. There was that dark richness to it, now. There were levels of meaning in it, shades and complications.

Or maybe that was just her poor, battered, traitorous heart.

She didn't argue with him any further. She didn't tell him that *of course* she worried, and he should worry, too. That nothing good could come of this. That whatever she might feel, she was still her father's daughter.

That her father would destroy them both, and her sister, without a second thought, and neither one of them could prevent it—or they already would have, surely.

That they were doomed.

But it was as if he heard her arguments all the same. He smoothed a hand over her hair, and that stern mouth of his even softened in the corners.

"Don't worry," Orion said, but to her, it sounded like a curse. And then he made it worse. "I trust you."

CHAPTER NINE

DECEMBER WORE ON, drawing ever closer to the twenty-third and the board meeting Calista still had every intention of disrupting.

Her father might have removed her from the office, but that didn't change all the things she'd spent years putting into motion. She told herself it was better that she was away from the company these last, critical days— because she was sure it would have been impossible to keep herself under control and seemingly subservient, the way she needed to do until it was done.

Calista spent these weeks in the palace rather than directly under her father's thumb. Not that she felt free of him, with the daily messages and calls demanding she provide him with dirt on Orion. Instead of spending her days at Skyros Media, fighting tooth and nail in meetings and building up her position behind her father's back, she found herself at the mercy of the king's private secretaries. She got a crash course in the Idyllian Crown and the duties of the king's consort, and spent hour after hour learning all the various facts they thought she needed to know—and they thought she needed to know just about everything.

In many ways, it reminded her of being back at university in Paris, sitting in endless lectures. But instead of producing essays out of café nights and too much red wine, she had to sit there and prove to them that she'd internalized their teachings on everything from international diplomacy to proper correspondence, all while fending off her father's demands.

Hour after hour after hour. Until she thought that if the whole queen thing didn't work out, she could easily become a professional historian. With a focus on Idyllian royals throughout the ages.

She should have been crawling out of her skin. She should have been beside herself, and she...wasn't. Or not in the way she'd expected she ought to have been, anyway.

Her days were spent immersed in history.

But her nights… Her nights were filled with Orion, and she almost couldn't bear to let herself think about what that meant.

"I don't understand how you never…" she'd whispered one night when they both lay panting before the fire in her bedchamber. "I don't understand anything about you."

"I made a vow," he'd replied lazily, turning her over on her belly and applying himself to the line of her back, turning her to jelly.

"You broke that vow, then."

She'd felt his smile against her skin and had shuddered. "I vowed I would only indulge in the pleasures of the flesh with my queen, Calista. I have broken no vows. Nor shall I."

And even now, weeks later, she almost couldn't bear to think about such moments, because thinking about them would mean analyzing them. Making decisions. And inevitably ruining these oddly bright weeks carved out in the darkest part of the year—and her life.

These weeks that made no sense. These weeks that made her doubt herself, her purpose, and everything she'd ever known.

All lit up and threaded through with Orion,

as if the king was his own holiday light and she glowed straight through. With him.

"Maybe you just like him," her sister said drily, a week before Christmas Eve. "Maybe he's likable. Maybe someday I'll actually get to meet him and decide for myself."

"You've met him."

"I was presented to him with half the kingdom in attendance at your engagement ball. Not the same thing."

Calista wasn't deliberately keeping Melody and Orion apart. But she also wasn't going out of her way to introduce them, either. She told herself there was no point. There were only six days remaining before the board meeting and seven days before her supposed wedding. Why pretend that her sister and Orion would ever need to interact?

Then again, here she was standing in one of the many palace salons, being pinned and sewed and otherwise fitted into a sweeping white gown she had no intention of ever *really* wearing. And certainly not for the ceremony it was being made for.

The palace advisers had decided, with very little input from Calista, that what was needed here was a fairy tale. The full Cinderella treatment, they called it, complete with a dress boasting skirts so wide she could have fit half the island beneath them, a tiny waist that stole her breath, and gold embroidered everywhere.

Just in case there was any doubt that she was marrying a king.

God help her, she was marrying *the king*.

No, she reminded herself. *You're only pretending you might.*

She seemed to keep forgetting that part.

"I'll take that as a yes," Melody said then, snapping her back to the salon. The dress. The disaster that was her life. "You do like him."

"I can't think of anything that matters less than *liking* someone," she replied, perhaps a bit grumpily. "Much less a person I'm being forced to spend time with."

The fleet of brisk seamstresses had left the room en masse ten minutes before, forced to contend with some or other textile disaster. They had spared Calista the details. She was left standing on a raised dais, surrounded by a portable wall of mirrors. Melody was there in the midst of it all, looking feral and entertained in the antique chair she'd claimed, and somehow more at home in this palace than Calista was.

"I would personally consider it a good thing that I liked a man I was going to have to marry even if he was a monster I detested," Melody said mildly. "But you do you, Calista."

Calista's hands were in fists, and she was glad her sister couldn't see it. Though the expression on Melody's face made her think that she knew, anyway. The way she always did.

"I have a plan," she began, trying to keep her voice even.

"It's not the end of the world if you change your plans," Melody interrupted her, quietly. "Maybe it's even for the best. There are opportunities everywhere, if you know how to look for them."

Calista opened her mouth to snap something back at her, but then paused. She frowned. "Are you talking about you or me?"

Melody smiled with a certain edge. "Father has been talking to me about alternate living opportunities."

Such a simple sentence, yet it sent cold water straight down Calista's back.

She knew she should have found something to feed to her father. Some bit of palace dirt. Some terrible rumor. How had she imagined that she could keep fobbing him off? Ignoring his messages and acting as if she was too busy with the wedding he'd demanded to give him what he wanted?

The truth was, she'd been pretending—hoping maybe, or wishing—that if she ignored the mess she was in, it might go away.

This was their father's way of reminding Calista what he was prepared to do.

What he had every intention of doing.

How could she have been so stupid?

"I knew this would happen." And suddenly the enormous dress she wore felt like a cage. A prison, and she couldn't breathe, and Calista didn't know what would happen if she simply clawed the fabric off her body—

Breathe, she ordered herself.

But she couldn't. Not really. Not with any depth.

"I think it will be fine, actually," Melody said, sounding philosophical. "I've never been around any other blind people. I might like them. At the very least, I can learn... blind things. Whatever those are."

Calista tried to breathe. She really did try. "This is all my fault."

"I think you know it's not, Calista. I think you know that the only reason I wasn't shunted off into one of these schools at birth is because of you."

Her sister sounded calm. Resigned.

Calista was anything but. "I've been so wrapped up in what was going on here." In sex, she thought, ashamed of herself. In *glowing.* "I should have known that they would make their move. I'm surprised they haven't done it already."

Calista wanted to tear down the walls. Shatter all the mirrors—but she was still trapped in her damned fairy-tale dress.

"Melody—" she began, her voice hot with guilt and shame.

But she stopped herself, because the door swung open.

And instead of the officious seamstresses who liked to stream in and out, issuing instructions, measuring things, and clucking around as if they really were all that wildlife in a Cinderella film, a man stood there.

Calista's heart kicked at her, but it wasn't Orion.

Why did she want it to be Orion?

In her chair, Melody shifted in that way she always did, instinctively hiding the truth about herself. Not the fact that she couldn't see, but that she wasn't helpless. She was good at it. She instantly looked smaller. Fragile and pathetic, even.

"Prince Griffin," Calista said, and it cost her something to sound calm. To pretend that she wasn't about to explode into pieces, right where she stood.

"Lady Calista," Griffin replied in that smooth way of his that Calista normally objected to, on principle. It was too pat. Too practiced. But he was shifting, looking over to where Melody made a pretty little picture of a damsel in distress in the corner.

It would have been laughable, really, if any of this had been something to laugh about.

"Your Royal Highness," Calista said, because she knew her etiquette now, backward and forward, whether she wanted to or not, "may I present to you my sister, Lady Melody."

Melody did not rise from her chair and sink into the appropriate curtsy, but she did bow her head in such a way that she gave the impression of doing it.

While Calista watched her soon-to-be brother-in-law as he did a set of rapid calculations, clearly recalling that this was the so-called "imperfect" Skyros sister.

"I am enchanted," he murmured, executing a perfect bow that Melody couldn't see. Though she likely heard it.

"Have you come to aid with the dress fitting?" Calista asked, glaring at him, because she could see him just fine. "In all the tales of your exploits, I've never heard anyone mention that you were good at dressing women. More the opposite."

"Not at all," Griffin said, and when he shifted that gaze of his back to her, Calista straightened. Because he looked lazy enough, with that half smile and the languid way he held himself. But that dark look in his eyes was anything but. "I came to warn you."

"Warn me?" Calista asked lightly.

She watched her sister in the mirrors. Melody was basically a parody of herself at this point, managing to look like the Little Match Girl. When she was perched on a brocaded chair that might as well have been a throne, here in the middle of the palace. Not out in a cold gutter.

It was quite a performance. It always was.

"The standard warning, really," Griffin said, sounding jovial. "We are all of us adults. And we understand the ways of our world, I assume. But I must tell you that if you wound my brother in any way, *he* will be the least of your concerns."

He sounded so polite. Almost apologetic. It took a moment for the words to penetrate.

"I can't wait for Melody to warn off the king in the same fashion," Calista replied.

"That's between your sister and the king." Griffin smiled wider. "If she wishes to threaten him, that is. Most people might avoid taking that route. As it is against the law."

"No need to worry about what I might do," Melody said, in a frail, tremulous sort of voice that made that tight vise around Calista's chest lighten a bit and she fought to keep herself from laughing. "I would never dare speak in the exalted presence of His Majesty."

Calista expected Griffin to smile in that strained, pitying way people usually did. To fail to see Melody as anything more than a bit of furniture, and more drab than the average chair.

This was Idylla's Playboy Prince, who was spared the hatred aimed at his father because he was always so charming. Not because he was any different.

But instead of dismissing and demeaning the version of herself Melody was offering him, Griffin…changed. He stood a little straighter. He stopped smirking. He looked at Melody, tiny and pathetic, and the expression on his face was almost…

Surely not, Calista thought.

"He is only a man," he said. "Flesh and blood, Lady Melody. No more and no less, no matter what manner of crown adorns his head."

Melody quailed as if the idea floored her. "If you say so, Your Royal Highness."

"Call me Griffin," he said, his attention on her younger sister in a way Calista could not say she liked. At all. It made the tiny waist of her gown seem even tighter. Especially when he kept going in that silken voice of his. "After all, we are practically family, are we not?"

Calista knew her sister well enough to see that description didn't sit well with her, even as she...fluttered. But if she wanted to play this game of hers, pretending she was a helpless creature at every opportunity when she wasn't, Calista was more than happy to go along with it. Particularly if it also slapped at Prince Griffin and his *warnings*.

"Hush now," she murmured soothingly. "This is part of why I'm marrying, Melody. To give you these wonderful new brothers."

And it was worth it when Melody forgot herself for a moment, focusing her whole body in Calista's direction with what seemed like obvious fury to her.

But Griffin was none the wiser. That was what mattered.

He was far too busy looking from Melody to Calista as if the word *brother* was a vile curse.

"I cannot wait," he murmured, all silk and seduction.

But Calista thought there was something else in his gaze as he took himself out of the room.

And for a moment, the sisters stayed where they were.

"It really is like a fairy tale," Calista said merrily. "Your very own Prince Charming cannot wait to welcome you to the family, Melody, despite your simpering."

"I really ought to kill you. You know I can, right?" Melody was no longer assuming her Little Match Girl persona. She looked like herself again, capable and intent. "With my own two hands."

"Yes, yes," Calista said and sighed. "But then what would become of either one of us?"

Melody laughed, settling back against her chair. As if it was all a joke.

But Calista knew better.

Her father was calling her bluff in this game she'd never wanted to play. She had six days left before she could make her move and she had no doubt that if she didn't throw him a bone, he would cart Melody off to some hor-

218 CHRISTMAS IN THE KING'S BED

rible prison of an institution somewhere. He'd call it a wedding present.

How could she live with that? Calista knew she couldn't. She had to make a decision, soon. And it shouldn't have been a hard one.

Of course she would protect her sister. The way she always had.

And she would do it at the expense of the man she'd never wanted to marry and shouldn't have let herself care for.

Even if it killed her.

CHAPTER TEN

TWO WEEKS LATER, Orion still could not explain why it was he'd chosen to tell Calista that she was his first.

His only.

Or better yet, why she was the only thing on this planet that could make him break a vow he'd kept even when he was half-mad with adolescent hormones.

He'd rationalized it away, of course. He had always said he wouldn't touch a woman unless he married her, and he was going to marry her. He would be making new and better vows in a week's time, come Christmas Eve. But he was entirely too aware that he was excusing himself in a way he would not excuse anyone else had they been in the same position.

The trouble was, hypocrisy was entirely too delicious.

A notion that forced him to reassess the

judgments he'd so happily levied on every other human alive. Like his father.

It was a particularly shattering thing indeed, to find himself feeling even vaguely compassionate about King Max. He hardly knew what to do with it.

Maybe it was easier to concentrate on his own sins, in the form of the woman he should not have touched—but he had.

Every morning for the past two weeks, he had woken with Calista. Tangled up in her bed, eyes gritty from lack of sleep, because after holding himself back from the pleasures of the flesh for so long, he was insatiable.

And she was nothing short of a feast. An endless banquet.

He could not get enough.

And because of her, Orion understood things he hadn't before. The magic of touch. The madness of wanting anyone that much, of thinking it might cause actual, physical pain to go without. The things he longed for now could all be wrapped up with a bow and called *more*.

He wanted to be closer. He wanted to ignore every last responsibility in his life and focus only on the things they could do to each other in that bed.

Perhaps the word he was searching for when he thought about Calista was *humbled*.

She made him all too aware that the only reason he had ever been able to wrap himself in his upright, moralistic cloak of self-righteousness was because he hadn't met her yet.

"You're staring at me again," she said, archly, from beside him. They were packed into yet another royal vehicle, en route to the last Christmas ball they would attend as an engaged couple.

Because next week's ball on the night before Christmas would be their wedding reception.

He wasn't sure he could name the way that beat in him, these days. He felt…possessive. Impatient. Because it was one more way to have her, and he intended to make sure he collected them all. Every last possible way there was to make her his, he intended to do it.

There was just this last week to get through.

"Can I not behold the woman who will be my wife?" he asked idly.

He held her hand in his, as had become his habit. He could not seem to keep himself from toying with the ring he'd put there, that great and glorious symbol of the queens of his people. And Calista was the last, best queen, by his reckoning. "In a mere week, Calista. Seven short days."

She glanced at him, and as ever, he saw that tension in her. A kind of wariness in her expression, but warmth in her gaze.

He chose to concentrate on the warmth.

And if he felt a kind of drumming intensity, as if they were hurtling toward an end he couldn't foresee—well. He chose to concentrate on the fact she would be his wife. Above all else.

"I can't decide if you're counting down to the day of our wedding with joy or if it's all become a bit dire," she said then, sounding almost muted. "Remember, Orion. You are being blackmailed into doing this."

"Did you imagine I might have forgotten that?" He never forgot it. Though he was aware that somewhere in his mind, he had separated Calista from her father. Aristotle was the person blackmailing him. Maybe that made Calista innocent. Maybe he only wished it did. "I assure you, it is never far from my thoughts."

"I can't say I understand you."

Tonight she looked particularly beautiful, but then, every time he saw her it was as if she'd transformed before his very eyes. There was a point at which he wasn't certain he would be able to look at her directly. That was how much she seemed to glow, brighter than the coming Christmas.

"What is there to understand?" he asked.

"You can't possibly trust me." She sounded outraged by the notion. "It's not possible. I'm the daughter of your enemy, and—"

"You are the daughter of my blackmailer, yes," he said. "But your father is not my enemy, Calista. How can a parasite be an enemy? It can only be what it is. A leech, nothing more."

She did not look mollified.

"The first day we met, I told you exactly who I was," she bit out, and Orion was astonished to see her eyes were stormy. "I made it clear that no matter what happened, I would never be on your side. Did you forget that?"

"It's not that I forgot it. It's that things changed."

"Things have changed for you." She sounded desperate.

And the truth was, Orion deeply enjoyed her desperation in all its forms. The fact that he could make her beg when she was naked. The sounds she made, the pleas and the sobs. He had never heard any music he liked more.

Even if this had a harder edge, it was possible he was enjoying it more than he should have.

"Is this another patronizing discussion about my virginity?" he asked, amused. "A casual observer might note that you seem… obsessed."

She pulled her hand from his, but not before he felt the tremor in it. "I'm not obsessed with it. I just think that it's entirely possible that the experience of losing it has affected you more than you imagine. Sex is just sex, Orion. It doesn't mean anything. It certainly doesn't mean that you should trust someone who's never given you any reason to do anything of the kind."

"Here's what I wonder," he said in a low

voice, watching her closely. If he wasn't mistaken, her eyes were slicked with an emotion he knew she would have denied. "What would happen if you worried less about what you thought *might* happen, and more attention to what actually has?"

"That's what I'm trying to tell you. Nothing has actually happened."

"I told you," he said. "I trust you."

She winced as if he'd hit her. "Then you're a fool."

And the way she said that, as if it was torn from her, haunted him as they pulled up into the line of cars delivering Idyllian nobles and commoners alike into the rest of their evening. Tonight's ball was held in a sprawling villa on the far end of the island. Held for centuries by one of Idylla's noble families, it had at different points in history been considered something of a secondary, southern palace.

This was usually Orion's favorite ball. The villa was a work of art, marrying Idyllian architectural prowess with Italianate and Hellenic accents, as suited their position in the Aegean Sea. On a night that was cool by island standards, all the villa's many atriums were filled with glowing heaters, strong lights. The imported evergreens were trimmed and bursting with ornaments. Night-blooming jasmine wafted in the air.

He and Calista were announced to the crowd and then led on a bit of a promenade through all the villa's public rooms, as was tradition, but all Orion could concentrate on was the woman by his side. That odd gleam in her gaze. And the desperation that he knew, deep down perhaps he'd always known, had nothing to do with him.

He pulled her out onto the dance floor in the largest of the ballrooms to lead off the first song.

Was it his imagination, or did she seem more brittle than usual? More fragile?

Even...scared?

She is none of those things, something in him whispered. *You should know better.*

But this wasn't about *knowing.* This was about *feeling.* And he suspected that if he said as much, she would bite his head off, there and then.

Still, that didn't change the fact she looked haunted.

"You could always tell me what's wrong," he said quietly, holding her so she had no choice but to tip her head back and meet his gaze. "I am the king. If I cannot help you, who can?"

Calista had her usual public smile on her face, but the look in her beautiful sea-colored eyes was pure misery. "There are some things even a king can't help."

"Is it so terrible, then?"

"Orion. There's no point in this."

"There is." He held her tighter, and recognized—yet again—that when it came to her he was not as in control as he should have been. Not even close. "Because I have to think that the woman I met in my private salon all those weeks ago would not have been torn. Whatever else she had going for her, chief among them was her sense of purpose. Maybe you should ask yourself, my lovely queen-to-be, what has happened to yours."

He didn't expect her eyes to darken the way they did. With a flash of temper and vulnerability that made him want nothing more than to gather her in his arms and carry her from this place, where so many eyes were upon them, and the glare of so much public interest made it hard for him to see her at all.

"I ask myself that question every day," Calista said, her voice thick and rough.

And then the dance was done, and it was back again to the endless rounds of glad-handing and stilted conversations it was his job to make smooth.

Ever since Orion had found her out there in a distant corner of the Botanical Gardens with her father, she'd stayed close. Tonight was no exception. She stayed right there at his elbow, graceful and obliging, everything his queen should be.

He was getting used to having her there, Orion could admit. And he would never have imagined that as a possibility, so used was he to doing everything by himself. But over these past weeks, Calista had bloomed into her role—whether she liked it or not. And the more she did, like the sweet jasmine in the air all around them, the more Orion began to comprehend what it would be like if he and his queen were really, truly some kind of team.

She was nothing like his mother, who had always looked wan and pale, as if the slightest impertinence might send her into a swoon.

Calista was not delicate. She was vibrant. Just amusing enough, without being flippant. Capable of gentle flattery and asking surprisingly incisive questions with that same sweet smile.

"If you're going to betray me," Orion said as he escorted her from one set of careful, diplomatic conversations to the next, "I wish you would hurry up and do it. Then we could put it behind us and move on."

"I had no idea you were such an optimist, Your Majesty," she said, her voice a mild reproof. Though there was something bitter beneath it. "From a distance, you always appear so stern."

"There could be no point in dedicating myself to changing this kingdom for the better if I lacked optimism," he said. "How could there be? The country is bloated with enough cynicism as it is."

Again, the look she gave him was dark. It made something in him tighten, as if in foreboding.

"Optimism is a privilege," she said quietly. "A gift."

Orion did not have time to chase that up as she moved to talk with a group of foreign ambassadors. Nor would he have, in all likelihood, even if they hadn't been in public— because there was a part of him that didn't want to know what ate at her.

A part of him that was afraid he did know, more like.

Still, if they were alone, he would have kissed her. He would have reached her that way.

Sometimes he thought it was the only way he *could* reach her.

Because he was certain, deep in his bones in a way he was not sure made any sense, that if he could simply marry Calista, everything would be all right. Making her his queen would break whatever spell it was that made her eyes go dark, as if this really was a fairy tale, after all.

Complete with its own ogre, he thought darkly when he found himself face-to-face with Aristotle.

Even though he had instructed his handlers

at length that was never to happen. He shot a hard look at the aide to his right, who leaned in with his usual deferential smile.

"I beg your pardon, sire," the man murmured in Orion's ear. "He claimed he would cause a scene if he did not get an audience with you."

And no doubt he would, Orion knew. No doubt he would make it into an opera, and happily. It was far better to suffer a conversation with Aristotle than to have to clean up another one of his messes.

But Orion didn't have to like it.

"Do you really think you can avoid me?" The other man snarled, his flat eyes gleaming in a way Orion really didn't like. "Surely you must know it doesn't work that way. I'm marrying my daughter to you for access."

"And here I thought I was marrying your daughter for damage control. Did we not sign documents to that effect?"

"Either way I will be your father-in-law. Your family, like it or not. And that must mean I will have the king's ear."

"No one is preventing you from speaking," Orion replied evenly. "As to whether or not I plan to take your advice, I think you already know the answer."

"You'd better watch yourself there, Your Majesty," the older man growled, in a way that moved in Orion unpleasantly. He felt his stomach clench. "You may have wrapped me up in legal nonsense concerning that portfolio. But there's more than one way to skin a cat."

Two months ago, it would not have occurred to Orion to consider how satisfying it would be to punch Aristotle in his round face. Tonight, he had to fight to keep himself from it—and succeeded only because the last thing Idylla needed was their king in a common brawl.

"I am not a cat," he said icily. "I am your king. And if I were you, Aristotle, I would endeavor to remember that before your mouth gets you into trouble."

His aide was not close enough to hear his words, but his tone must have carried, because the man winced.

Aristotle snorted. "You are king of an island," he sneered. "But I am king of a far greater kingdom. I tell people how to think.

I tell them what to feel. I make up stories and convince them it's the truth. All you do is wave from the back seat of a car, or wink invitingly on a few commemorative plates."

"A person with so little respect for the monarchy should not be quite so desperate to marry into it, I would have thought," Orion replied, keeping his voice cool—but wholly unable to do much about the edge beneath it.

"I made a meal of your father and the fact he couldn't keep his pants on," Aristotle said, looking smug and entirely…satisfied. "What do you think I'll make out of a grown man as inexperienced as you are?"

For a moment, it was if everything—the villa, the world, all of creation—went blank.

Calista.

Her name was a cry inside him. A curse.

But she had already told him what she'd done, Orion realized, as if from a great distance.

She'd told him and she'd told him again, and he hadn't listened.

It shouldn't have surprised him—shocked him, even—that she had told him she would betray him, and then had.

He just hadn't expected it to take this form.

"If I have a king in my pocket," Aristotle was crowing at him, "you can bet that I have my own daughter sewed up tight. You need to adjust your attitude, sire."

And then the vile little man swaggered away from him, leaving Orion to stand there.

Stunned.

With no one to blame but himself.

CHAPTER ELEVEN

"SOMETHING MUST BE the matter," Calista said, when a solid half hour had passed in brooding silence. The drive from the far southern tip of the island to the royal city, and the palace, took almost two hours.

And she had never known Orion to be so quiet, when he was not tending to his many messages. Or more accurately, to go without speaking.

Because he might not be using words, but he was not particularly *quiet* at all. On the contrary, he seemed to be burning up as he sat there beside her seemingly staring out the window at nothing. White hot and loud.

"A great many things are the matter," he replied then, surprising her. "But none of them require conversation."

And the tone he used made her chest…hurt.

"What did my father say?" she asked, because she'd seen them, off to the side in a little alcove, where no one else could hear. And she knew full well how her father liked to take advantage of things when no one else could hear him.

She felt a clock ticking inside her, so loud that her head ached.

Time is running out, something within her whispered.

Because somehow, she'd forgotten that the point of all of this was Melody. Taking her father's power so that he couldn't hurt Melody. It was Orion's fault. He had made her feel things she would have said she didn't believe in—

But none of that mattered. It couldn't matter, not until the board meeting was done. On December 23, she would take on her father, and win. At last.

Even if, inside, it felt as if she'd already lost.

It doesn't matter how it feels, she snapped at herself. *It matters that you get it done so Melody is never at risk again.*

"What do you imagine your father had to say to me?" Orion asked, and for the first time in this interminable car ride, he actually angled his head to look at her.

The breath left her in a harsh exhalation she could do nothing to prevent.

Because for the first time, possibly ever—and certainly in as long as she'd known him—King Orion looked…

Furious.

"I've no idea," she gritted out, though that was a lie, and her heart was galloping.

"I blame myself," he said in a gritty sort of voice that didn't make anything better. "After all, you did warn me. Repeatedly. But somehow, I thought your loathing of your father would win the day."

She tried to make her heart stop racing. "Everybody loathes my father. He inspires it in everyone. I'm not sure that's newsworthy."

"Understand this," Orion told her then, his voice a hard thing and his dark gold gaze pinning her to her seat. "I am not embarrassed by my inexperience. If it were splashed across every paper in the land, I would not care at all. I kept my vows of celibacy because I wanted to keep them, and I broke them because I wanted to break them. You and your father cannot shame me with the truth."

His name was on her lips, but she bit it back. She didn't dare.

Orion held that terrible gaze on hers. "What shames me, Calista, is that I imagined you were better than him."

Calista felt sick.

She hated herself, deeply and wildly, and she hated most of all that she'd felt she had no choice but to throw her father a bone. Because she had to keep him happy and distracted or she knew she would never see her sister again. He would ship her off somewhere, never tell her where, and if Calista was lucky, she might get upsetting reports about how Melody was faring from time to time.

It was more likely that he would act as if Melody had never existed, just to torture Calista.

She could see it all unfold before her as if it had already happened.

The decision should have been an easy one. She hated that it hadn't been. That telling her father something so private had made her feel as dirty and disgusting as he was.

It had never occurred to her that he would

sell her out so quickly. Not before the wedding, anyway.

"I had no choice," she said now, trying not to sound as miserable as she felt.

"No attempts to convince me it wasn't your fault, I see. No tears, no protestations."

She lifted her chin, even though there wasn't a single part of her that didn't want to curl into a ball and die. "I think you know that my father delivered me into your hands for one reason only. To funnel information back to him."

He let out a hollow laugh. "Why did I imagine otherwise?"

"I don't believe you did," she made herself say, as if nothing had changed between them from that first meeting to now. "Not really."

Another laugh, as if he was angry at himself, not her. Or perhaps both. "It is good to know that you follow instructions to the letter, Calista. Something I will have to keep in mind in the future."

She wanted to cry. She wanted to hit things, or possibly just crawl away somewhere and sob her heart out.

Instead, she made herself glare at him. "I

warned you. I told you not to trust me. There was no reason why you should have in the first place."

And her heart stuttered in her chest when he reached over and took her chin in his fingers.

"Because I wanted to trust you, Calista," he bit out. "Because I knew exactly who you were, but I hoped—I wished—that you might surprise yourself."

"Then you really are a fool," she threw back at him, though it made her shake. "What did you imagine? That you could change the world simply because you decreed it?"

She jerked her chin out of his fingers, but she was all too aware that he let her go. And more, that she wished he hadn't.

"Yes," Orion said, starkly. "I thought you would want to change."

He couldn't have hurt her more if he'd swung and hit her.

Hard.

Her breath left her as if he had.

"You will never know how much I wanted—"

But Calista cut herself off, because it was all futile. It didn't matter. This was never the part of her life that was supposed to matter. This was the distraction, and she didn't understand when or how the King of Idylla had shifted everything around inside her.

When he had got to her and got her so… *muddled.*

Some mornings, she woke up and forgot all about board meetings and Skyros Media and her lifelong dream of bringing down her father.

For hours.

And every time she remembered, it was another betrayal of her sister.

She couldn't pretend she hadn't known, when she'd chosen to give her father information about Orion—much less *that* information—that she was sacrificing those hours of freedom, no matter how much she'd loved to forget the mess of it all. The squalid dirt that had made her family's name.

She knew full well she was sacrificing the bright glow of these past weeks for the same cold future she'd always been aiming toward.

It was the right thing to do, she told herself, again and again. A king would always prosper, but the same couldn't be said of Melody, there beneath their father's thumb.

But that it was right didn't make it hurt less.

Calista was starting to think that the hurt was a part of it, and one more price she would have to pay.

Sometimes, looking at him, it almost felt worth it.

"I don't understand any of this," she said, trying to keep her eyes away from him in the shadows of the back seat, because it was too painful. But it didn't work. "You and I should never have met. You should never have told me that you were a virgin. All of this could have been avoided if you'd stood up to my father in the first place. It wasn't your sin. It was your father's."

She shook her head, terribly afraid that the sobs that caught in the back of her throat might pour out now, whether she wanted them to or not. She felt jagged and broken and *hurt*, and she didn't have the slightest idea what to do about any of it.

"You're the bloody king, Orion. Surely you could have made this—made *him*—go away."

His mouth twisted, and there was something so savage in his eyes then it made her heart skip a beat.

"It's not my father's sins that worry me," he belted out. "It's my mother's."

She gaped at him. He muttered something that might have been a curse, then dragged his hands over his face. Then he pressed the button that allowed him to talk to his driver and ordered the man to pull over to the side of the road.

When the car stopped, Orion threw open the door and the sea rushed in.

Calista was breathing too hard. As if she'd been running all the way down the long island road from the villa instead of sitting in his car.

And she didn't want to follow him out. She didn't want to hear any more of his secrets. Because she'd told him he couldn't trust her, but worse than that, she didn't trust herself.

She was terrified, not that he would tell her more secrets that she would feel compelled to tell her father.

But that he would tell her enough of his secrets that she *wouldn't* share them with her father.

And Melody would pay the price.

What would any of this have been for?

Calista could hear the crash of the winter sea against the rocks. She told herself that was what lured her out, crawling carefully from the car and closing the door behind her. And taking a moment, then, to lean against the side of the vehicle and wait for her eyes to adjust.

When they did, the stars were so bright in the night sky above her it took her breath away.

And when she angled her gaze away from the resplendent sky, it was to see Orion standing there on a flat rock overlooking the rocky shore, like a dark dream made real.

She was as drawn to him now as ever, she understood with a little jolt inside, no matter if it was against her will. Especially now he knew exactly how perfidious she was. The lengths she was willing to go.

The betrayer she'd become to fight a man who had made her in his image after all. Because all the *whys* didn't matter. She'd sold Orion out.

Though, tonight, all the things she'd been

telling herself for years to keep herself focused on felt flat inside her. Like paltry little excuses.

In order to save one person who mattered to her she'd lost another.

She didn't know how she was meant to live with that.

He didn't turn around to see what she was doing, and maybe that was why she felt so drawn to him. His certainty. How sure he was of himself, so that when he'd actually made love for the first time in his life, she would have sworn that he'd had decades of experiences.

She had let him get close to her. Close enough to shame her, and she didn't know how she was supposed to cope with that. How she was supposed to carry on doing what she'd always done when she knew that this sickening current of self-disgust could just… bloom inside her the way it did?

"I'm sorry," she whispered when she reached him.

But the December wind, cool enough to make her shiver, if not cold in any real sense, took her words away.

Orion was staring out at the dark water, as if he was fighting his own battle while standing still.

"What your father has on me is a portfolio of pictures," he told her, matter-of-factly. As if it was part of some royal decree.

"You don't have to tell me anything," Calista said, feeling wretched. "Surely by now you should know better than to want to."

"It's an old roll of film, with twenty-four exposures. The portfolio contains both prints and negatives. Your father assured me that no copies had ever been made."

"Even if there were, he likely would have found them and destroyed them," she said, clearing her throat as she thought about the squalid little bargains Aristotle called "business." "Because the value in a damaging image is lessened if there are copies. If anyone can have leverage, the leverage itself is lessened."

She felt her face go hot when Orion slanted a look her way. "Yes, these are the sorts of things I learned at my father's knee. Don't act so surprised, Orion. Surely you didn't think he sang us nursery rhymes?"

"The images are quite standard, really," Orion continued, darkly. "King Max engaged in yet another threesome. But in this case, the photos feature the king and another man focused on particular shared acts. And the woman in question…"

He didn't finish his sentence.

"No," Calista whispered.

"The woman in question is my mother," Orion gritted out, as if it hurt him. And that fury in him was a raw and pulsing thing. "She looks enthusiastic, but also as if that enthusiasm was chemically enhanced. And I can tell you that in the days leading up to her death—which, according to the date stamped on these pictures, was not long after the event—she would drink too much and say a great many things that made no sense. Then. They make more sense now."

"Orion…"

"She was concerned about gaps in her memory. She was…fragile, and she refused to eat or drink anything she did not prepare herself. I can only assume now that she was given something in her food or drink that was laced with the sort of drugs that create enthusiasm where there is none."

Calista let that sink in, though it made her stomach lurch. "And you think it was your father…?"

"Does it matter?" His voice was a vicious slap against the wind. "Whether my father slipped her a drug to make her compliant, or merely took advantage of it when he must surely have known better—does it really matter which? What *degree* of monster he was? And as I allow my outrage and sickness over this to turn around inside me, I must ask myself why it is that every other photo I've ever seen with him in various sexually explicit scenarios, I never questioned the enthusiasm of the participants. Only when it suited me."

"Because your poor mother…"

"Yes. My poor mother."

Orion shook his head, looking sick and furious and tired, suddenly. It made the rocks beneath Calista's feet seem to sway, because this was *Orion*. He *was* the rock, and it had never occurred to her that he could go weary.

It made her want to fight anything that might come at him, even if it was her.

"I'm not even certain that the kingdom would bother to react to yet another explicit photograph of my father," he said after a moment or two. "But I cannot bear to think of my mother being tarred with the same brush. Not to mention, the fact that there are pictures of one such event would lead to the inevitable speculation that it was not a one-off. And that would lead to questions about parentage. Bloodlines."

"You can't have that," she whispered, flushing with a shame so deep and hot she was surprised she could still stand.

"The truth of the matter, Calista, is that I am sick unto death of the excesses of my father's reign," Orion said, and she had never heard him sound so dark. She had never felt that darkness inside her, too. "I felt this way before it affected my direct family and I only feel it more strongly now. And yes, I am willing to marry the daughter of a man who trafficked in those photographs to prevent them ever getting out. I still am. Whatever that makes me."

Calista thought it made him a hero. Possibly even a saint.

She was afraid to put words to what it made her.

"I wish..." Her tongue felt thick in her mouth. She had no idea what to say, only that everything hurt and she hated herself. And this, because after a lifetime of being certain that she was nothing like her father, she was. She'd proved it. Maybe she had different reasons, but the end result was the same. "I thought I wasn't tainted by him. But he is like an infection in the blood. It doesn't go anywhere. It will only twist in you until it wrecks you, over time."

"That is a choice." Orion's voice was clipped and harsh, but his eyes blazed. "Do you think I don't know the temptation to become just as dark and dissipated as the man who bore me? Do you think I don't ask myself daily if it would have been easier to follow in his footsteps? It's a *choice*, Calista. You have chosen to become your father. That's on you, not him."

"You don't understand."

"Then tell me."

And the most astonishing thing by far was that he shouted that.

As if this was the same thing as what happened to him in that bed they shared.

King Orion Augustus Pax, losing control.

And this time, Calista took no satisfaction from it. This time, he made her shudder and feel like weeping, and not in any kind of delight.

"I—"

His hands were on her shoulders then. His face in hers.

"Do not tell me what you cannot do. Just do it, or do not." His grip tightened. "I have seen the tension in you from the very start. Did you think I would miss it somehow? You want so badly to be bulletproof. To care as little about the people you come into contact with as your father does. But you're not him, Calista. You don't have to do the things he does."

She felt that everywhere, half indictment, half wish.

She thought it might take her to her knees,

but his hands gripped her shoulders, and she stood.

Because like it or not, she always stood. And did the horrible things no one else could—no matter what it cost her.

"I have spent my entire life working hard to get myself into a position where I can change things," she heard herself say, as if she could possibly explain herself to this man she was terribly afraid she might love.

This man she had already betrayed.

"In a week, you will become capable of simply moving your little finger and changing whatever you like, as queen. Or did you forget that when you marry me, the only person with more power than you in all the world is me?"

"That doesn't count," she threw at him, feeling desperate and despairing, all at once. "That's what he wants. Don't you understand?"

"Are you concocting some doomed attempt to make your father feel things like a normal human being?" His eyes blazed still, that terrible gold. "From sad experience, Calista, I can tell you it won't work. I tried to talk to my father once, man-to-man. It only served to entertain him."

She let out a sound that was not quite a sob. "I don't want to *talk* to my father. I want to crush him."

"And then what?" Orion demanded, his fingers pressing into her skin. "When you rise to take his place, what will become of you?"

She shook her head, but it didn't occur to her to pull away from him. Not yet. Or maybe she couldn't.

Maybe, despite everything, she didn't want to.

How had this happened? How had she lost her focus so completely?

But she knew. It was him. It was Orion.

He had gotten beneath her skin, and worse, into her bones. She couldn't take a breath without feeling him there, and she knew there'd be no changing that. That no matter what happened here, or next week in her board meeting, or on Christmas Eve, or ever after, straight on into the future, he would stay right there.

Deep in her bones, always.

For good or ill.

The inevitability was almost comforting.

"What are you going to do?" he demanded, his beautiful face close.

She thought of all the years she'd put in. Her father's handprint on her face. Her sister, so fiercely herself despite her parents' horror that she had come out of the womb something less than perfect in their eyes.

"I will do what I have to," she said.

And understood as she did that this thing between them, these last two weeks, was only the latest thing she sacrificed on the altar of this quest of hers.

"Be certain this is what you want," Orion said, his voice like a bell deep inside her. He dropped his hands. "Because the truth, Calista, is that I am not so optimistic. No son of my father's could be. And when I stop hoping for better, that is when, I am afraid, you will find me far less accommodating and far more uncompromising than you can possibly imagine."

"Medieval," she whispered, remembering their first meeting. She cleared her throat. "You can imprison me on Castle Crag if you must, Orion. But it won't change anything. It can't."

"So be it," he whispered, and there was a finality in his voice.

And when he turned and headed back to the car, away from the sea, the ring she wore on her hand felt heavy. Like iron.

Like prison bars, close and tight around her.

You have no choice, she told herself, again and again. She had to keep Melody safe.

Maybe Orion was right, and once she became his queen—*if* she became his queen— she would find herself able to *decree* her sister safe... But what if her father acted before then?

She would risk herself. But she refused to risk her sister.

"I have no choice," she whispered, when there was only the December wind to hear.

And it seemed to her the sea itself laughed at her predicament, doused her in salt and recrimination, and then left her to the fate she'd made real with her own two hands.

CHAPTER TWELVE

ON THE NIGHT before his wedding, Orion stood in his office, there at the window with his back to the palace where he had always been most comfortable.

Not that anything could comfort him these days.

The royal city stretched out before him, the lights sparkling brighter than usual with holiday splendor, and more this year. Because tomorrow was the royal wedding, and the celebrating kingdom had no idea that their new king was anything but transported with joy at the prospect.

The way he might have been a week ago, it pained him to admit. And no matter the faintly sniffy headlines in some of the tabloids, which questioned the timeline the palace had given them about the king's romance.

He knew those headlines were warning shots.

But it was the word *romance* that sat in his chest like a spot of pneumonia, gnarled and heavy, and worse by the day.

He found no peace in this view tonight.

Because instead of the kingdom he planned to save, all he could see was Calista.

He had barely seen her since that fateful last ball, when he had discovered what he should already have known—that she was as devious and untrustworthy as her father. That she could have turned her back on Aristotle and his schemes, but had chosen not to.

That she had made those choices despite what had happened between them.

That whatever it was that haunted her, she refused to share it with him.

It was that last that bothered him the most, loathe as he was to admit it.

They had run into each other once in the hallway of the family wing. She had been surrounded by a pack of seamstresses all dressed in black, a wild sort of look on her face—until she saw him.

She had gone silent. Still.

Haunted straight through, something in

him had intoned, but he couldn't *help* her betray him.

A man—a king—had to draw the line somewhere, surely.

He had stared at her, not certain what he was meant to do with all the unwieldy *feelings* inside him, now. He had wanted nothing more than to be the opposite of his father. And instead, it turned out that while his temptations might not level the kingdom— they might just level him. They might just lay him out flat all the same.

Neither one of them had spoken.

He had inclined his head. She had performed the expected bob of head and knee upon one's first daily sighting of the monarch.

And he had wasted an entire day when he should have been sorting out cabinet ministers and putting out fires all over the kingdom, brooding about that interaction.

Another time, he'd heard her.

Calista and her sister, laughing together in one of the rooms where the staff was laying out her trousseau. He had stopped himself midstride, the sound of her laughter seeming to pierce straight through him.

He was an embarrassment to himself. A disappointment, certainly.

But none of that mattered as the days dragged by and he began to realize exactly what he was signing himself up for.

It had been better before. He had been fascinated, and that was far better than disappointed. He had to think that it was worse, now, to know how good it could be between them when it could never, ever be like that again.

He couldn't unknow it.

But he wasn't sure how he could live with it, either. Sometimes he would find himself in one of his meetings or ceremonies, suddenly seized with a kind of deep panic at the endless stretch of days before him. Days that would become months, then years. If he was lucky, he would keep this marriage of convenience civil, if chilly.

Year after year after year, as they both turned to stone.

Sooner or later, the vivid longing of these weeks would fade. He was sure of it. It would be like a dream he'd had once—never quite forgotten, but never repeated.

"You do not look quite the part of the happy bridegroom," came his brother's drawling voice from behind him.

Orion sighed, but turned to face him all the same. "Should I be turning cartwheels down the corridors of the palace?"

"Not looking murderous might be a start." Griffin's gaze swept over him. "Where is your lovely bride-to-be? Sequestered some-where around here, presumably? Surrounded by the usual passel of women and dreams of her special day, one assumes?"

Even if Calista had not been her father's weapon, she would still be Calista—but Orion did not allow himself to succumb to the urge to defend her. Not tonight.

"My bride-to-be has not shared her plans with me," Orion said instead. "Then again, I did not ask."

Griffin blinked at that, standing behind the chair he usually preferred to lounge in. Orion watched as his brother tapped his fin-ger against the back of the chair, as if con-templating something. Deeply.

The world must have ended.

"If you've come here to give me marital advice," Orion said softly, "don't."

Griffin smiled. Faintly. "What marital advice could I possibly have to give? The closest I've been to that blessed state was witnessing our parents' union. Not exactly the sort of thing that would turn a man's thoughts to marital bliss, was it?"

Orion's smile felt thin and mean on his mouth. "You have no idea."

"If you are holding on to something that affects us both, out of some misplaced sense of duty," Griffin replied, in much the same tone Orion had used, "I will remind you that I'm not a child."

Orion knew that too well. But he also knew that he could have quite happily lived out the rest of his life without knowing what had happened between his parents. Or what had caused his mother to make the choices she had.

Why should he ruin what scant good memories Griffin had, too? He didn't see the point.

"I will always do my duty," he said instead, and felt far more tired than he had when he'd used to make such statements. When they had been hopes and dreams instead of simple facts. "I made that promise to you years ago. And to the rest of the kingdom."

"Yes, yes," Griffin murmured. "No one doubts your commitment, brother. What I do wonder, though, here on the eve of your wedding to a woman so unworthy of you that it is almost laughable—"

"You are speaking of my queen," Orion growled, all steel and menace, and only then recalled that he did not plan to defend her. Not tonight. But he had already started, so he kept on. "I will not have it. Not even from you, Griffin."

His brother looked as if he wanted to laugh, but wisely did not.

Instead, he nodded. "Understood. But while you are busy being on her side, whether she deserves it or not, know that I'm on yours. And not because I want your job, because I don't. I never have and I never will."

"I am aware." Orion thought his voice was too harsh, then. Too rough, but he had lost the ability to moderate it. "It's maddening, if you must know the truth. Younger royal siblings are supposed to want nothing more than to usurp the heir's position, with all the usual sniping and backbiting."

"I would rather die."

Orion smiled despite himself. "This I know."

And the two of them looked at each other, then away. It might have been an embrace, had they been different men.

"Tomorrow I will stand at your side and welcome your new queen to our family and this kingdom," Griffin told him, his voice as solemn as his gaze was uncharacteristically serious. "I represent the entirety of the royal family besides you, and so I can say with certainty that she will be supported. As long as you wish it."

Orion thought of Calista. Beautiful, faithless Calista.

He thought of the betrayal she had already enacted, and the others that were sure to follow. And he had lied to Griffin. He knew that Calista was not in the palace tonight. He had been informed when she left and with a single phone call, he could determine where she was now—but did he really want to know?

Orion would have asked himself why he

was bothering to protect her, but, of course, he knew.

Because he loved nothing more than exercises in futility, particularly if it came with a side dose of martyrdom. Except possibly the one woman who had ever gotten beneath his skin.

But he said nothing of these things to his brother.

"I wish it," he said. "I want her supported, no matter what."

Griffin nodded. And turned to go, but Orion stopped him.

"But while we are discussing duties in support," he said.

"I promised you that I would do my bit to stabilize the kingdom," Griffin replied, a bit tightly. "I haven't forgotten."

"I'm glad to hear it. Part of why I'm getting married is so that there can be no more gossip. No more innuendo. No more dating, Griffin. No more scandalous exploits. The next woman you are connected with I will expect you to marry, do you understand me?"

He thought there was something in his

brother's gaze then. Griffin looked…arrested, perhaps.

But he only swallowed, hard. Then nodded.

"As you wish, brother," he said gruffly.

Orion turned again once Griffin left and found himself scowling out into the dark, past the lights of the city, down to where the nearly full moon danced along the waves of the Aegean.

The moonlight made a silvery path across the water, and he wished he could figure out a path through the mess this had all become as easily.

He had no idea how long he stood there, but when he heard the door to his office open again, he sighed.

"I have already told you," he began, turning with every expectation of finding his brother there again.

But it was not Griffin who stood there.

It was Calista.

For a moment his mind blanked out. At first glance, she looked cool, impenetrable. She wore a sleek corporate outfit that made his mouth water. A pencil skirt that hugged her figure and a silk blouse that showed absolutely nothing of her beautiful breasts, yet made him so hungry for a taste of them that he thought he might shake with need. Another pair of those gloriously high, impractically dangerous shoes that did things to her calves a man could have written whole sonnets about.

Even her blond hair was ruthlessly controlled, wrenched back into something conservative and appropriate.

She looked absolutely ruthless from head to toe—except for her eyes.

They were as aquamarine as ever, blue and green and wild tonight.

Hectic, even.

"What are you doing here?" Orion asked coolly. "I assumed you had already made your choice. A week ago."

She moved farther into the office, her hands clutching the strap of the bag over her shoulder, another sign that she was not as controlled as she wished to appear.

Though he dared not hope.

Hope had already gotten him in enough trouble.

"I did."

Calista stopped, there on the other side of his desk, and he watched as she swallowed. Hard. And hated the part of him—that terrible weakness in him—that wanted to vault over the desk and hold her to him, as if he could somehow protect her from danger when the danger was her.

"Then I assumed we would march into our royal marriage the way most do," he said, when it appeared she planned to say no more. "With cold reserve. A pretense of civility, when necessary. And after you provide me with an heir, we can repair to completely separate lives."

Orion told himself he was imagining the look of misery on her face then, the one that matched the misery in him at the very notion—because of course he was imagining it. Because any possibility of something different between them was gone. She had said so herself.

It was his burden to bear that he had broken his vow and lost himself in the process. He had the rest of his life to mourn his one and only loss of control.

Or to dream about it in Technicolor detail, more like, a voice in him whispered.

"Tonight I went to the Skyros Media offices for the annual board meeting," she told him, and he had the sense she was picking her words. That she was walking on eggshells he couldn't see.

He frowned. "I thought you were fired."

"From my position as vice president, yes." She nodded. "But years ago, in an effort to cheat more effectively on his taxes, my father transferred shares of the company to members of the family. My sister sold me hers long ago, for a single shiny penny. My mother gave me hers in a lovely show of entirely feigned maternal support when I was promoted to vice president, something she has long regretted. That gave me, in total, forty-five percent of the company. My father has never concerned himself about that, because I'm so obedient. A tool for him to use, as I believe you put it so succinctly."

She loosened her grip on the strap of her bag, and shifted it off her shoulder, then set it down on the desk that stood between them.

There were so many things Orion wanted

to say to her, but something about the too-still way she stood, and that look on her face, kept him from it.

"I have worked for years to get to this meeting," she told him, her voice quiet, but racked with some emotion he couldn't name. "And finally, after years and years of near misses, setbacks, and disappointments, it was all finally going to happen. I managed to convince just enough members of the board to throw their lot in with mine. That would put me at fifty-one percent. Meaning, a controlling interest in Skyros Media. My first act would be a vote of no confidence in my father, which he would not survive. I intended to reject him from his own company by the end of the year."

"Why?" Orion asked, his throat so tight he wasn't sure the word would come out right.

"Because I want my sister safe," Calista said fiercely. "That has always been my first and foremost priority. He has threatened me with her all my life. If I misbehaved, he would have her minders lock her in her room, without food. If he was truly angry at me, he might slap me—but he'd leave her black-and-blue. And if I didn't tell him what he wanted to know about you, Orion…" Her voice wavered then, but she lifted her chin. "He told me he would send her to an institution. For life. Kicking him out would mean substantially reducing the amount of time, money, and energy he can dedicate to bullying me and her."

"You are discussing the sister-in-law of the King of Idylla," Orion reminded her, raising his brows, even as a rush of sympathy moved in him for her predicament—when he would have said he could never forgive her for betraying him in the way she did. "I will make it a law, if you wish, that your sister must remain free." He shook his head. "Why did it not occur to you that all you needed to do was ask?"

"Because I was so close," she threw at him, and she sounded much less composed, then. "My whole life was leading to tonight, and I thought it was nothing more than a strange tangent that I was suddenly thrown in your path. What did I care if my father wanted to marry me off? Soon enough what he wanted wouldn't matter. I could break off our engagement. I could divorce you. I didn't really care what I did, when you were just a figurehead to me. Just a king. Not a person, Orion. And not when Melody was the one who would suffer if I lost focus."

He stayed where he was, every muscle in his body tense, focused on her so intently he should have been worried it would rip him asunder.

But all he could manage to think about was her.

"I never expected...you," Calista whispered. She looked away then, blinking rapidly. And he wondered if that sheen in her gaze was what he thought it was when she looked back at him again. When he was sure she would have sworn she never cried. "But then, last week, it seemed that everything was..."

"In ruins all around us?" he asked starkly.

"Clarified," she said instead. "However harshly. So tonight, I went to the board meeting. It was exactly as I imagined it. I arrived late, to make an entrance. There were the expected whispers and mutterings when I walked into the meeting and took my place.

My father looked apoplectic, because he expected me to be sequestered off in the palace, allowing him to cast my vote by proxy, as he preferred."

She sniffed. "Only once every few years has he allowed me to attend the meetings, so I could have the pleasure of voting the way he told me to, but in person. In some ways that is a gift, as this is the sort of meeting that goes on for hours and takes a long while to get to the voting. At the first break, I knew that if I stayed, my father would become abusive. As usual."

Orion heard himself growl. "The next time he puts his hands on you, Calista, there will be consequences."

Her lips twitched and something in him warmed at the site. That optimism that he claimed came and went—but, in truth, only hunkered down within him, waiting for its moment—burst to life all over again.

Like fireworks.

But he tried to tamp it all down and assume his usual stern expression.

"I didn't intend to give him the opportunity to put his hands on me," she assured him. "I ducked out the door and slipped away because I knew that he would get caught up in conversation, and I needed to ready myself for the final act of this thing. At last."

"Have you come here to tell me that you are breaking off our engagement?" Orion asked then, the fireworks starting to feel a bit more like gunfire. "I suppose I should thank you for doing it in person."

His mind spun out, then. He thought of the scandal it would cause. The crowing in the papers that as they'd suspected, the king had been played for a fool by a member of the toxic Skyros family. And, really, how could anyone esteem a king who was a fool? Better, really, to be a villain. At least there was power in it instead of pity.

But Calista was talking again. "I went and hid in my office. It's right next my father's, so I knew there'd be no particular rush for someone else to take it over. I left all the lights out and stood there, staring out at that very same moon."

"It is not quite full," he heard himself say. "It will be full tomorrow."

Again, that sheen in her gaze made his chest feel tight.

"There was something about the moon, full or not." She looked down at the ring on her hand. That ring he'd put there, and now could not imagine gracing any other hand, ever. Everything in him rejected the very idea. "It was as if the moon and the sea caught the stones. And they all twisted around and around inside me. And all I could think about was last week. When we stood in the dark, with only the sea and the rocks as witness, and you asked me to make a choice I was certain was already made."

"Was it not?" he hardly dared ask.

"I could hear it when they started calling the meeting back to order," she said, her voice barely above a whisper. A rough, harsh whisper, her eyes fixed on his. "And everything I had always wanted was in that boardroom. Mine for the taking. I could hear my father's voice, booming down the hall as he told one of his vile, off-color jokes. All I had to do was move. Turn on my heel, walk down the hall, and crush him beneath my foot the way I've always dreamed."

"Calista."

And then again, just her name, like a prayer.

"Instead, I went into his office." She sounded as if she was running, but she stood still, there on the other side of the old desk that had once been his grandfather's. "I went to his safe. It only took me three or four tries to guess his combination, because it never occurs to my father that anyone might be observing him. He thinks he's too busy studying everyone else, looking for weaknesses, for anyone to return the favor."

She looked down, then, and it felt like a slap. Orion blinked. But she was reaching into the bag she'd tossed on his desk. And she pulled out a very familiar portfolio.

Then she set it on the expanse of the desk between them tenderly, as if it was a bomb.

"Is that…?" But his pulse was going crazy in his veins. And he was staring at her as if she was a ghost, or the sun, or some beautiful, complicated combination of both. "Calista. You didn't."

"I made my choice," she whispered, her voice thick. "The board voted to remove him, but in the end, I knew my place wasn't there. It's here. With you."

And then, her eyes really did fill with tears.

More astonishing, she did nothing to hide them.

Orion had no memory of moving. But he was around his desk, with his hands on her, before his next breath was through.

"I want to be the woman you thought I was when you told me you could trust me," she cried, her head back and her face…open. Tears in her eyes and nothing but stark honesty stamped across her features.

And in all his life, Orion had never been so humbled.

"I want the future," she told him, her voice broken. "I want a future with you. I've spent my whole life battling the past, and it's done nothing but make me sick and slimy, just like him."

"Never," he growled.

"I want those weeks we shared to become our life," she continued, as if it scared her. But she kept going. "And I want you to know, Orion, that betraying you almost killed me. Because none of what happened between us was anything to me but sacred. And the thought that I destroyed it, forever, breaks my heart."

She pulled in a ragged breath that sounded like a sob. "So I've proved it to you the only way I could. By setting you free."

"Calista." He pulled her closer to him, holding her tightly, the way he wanted. The way he always wanted—he, who had taught himself not to want at all, until her. "I've already told you. You cannot shame me with the truth."

"I'm not ashamed of your truths," she sobbed. "I'm ashamed of *me*. I'm ashamed that it took me right up to the eleventh hour to understand what I was becoming."

"You were fighting fire with fire," he said, surging to her defense without stopping to think about it. The way he always would. "There's nothing wrong with that."

"You found another way." Her hands were braced against his chest and the way she looked at him made him feel like a god, not a king. "You always find another way. You never sink to anyone's level, you make your own."

"Of course I do," he said, and allowed himself a small hint of a smile. "I am the king."

"I only hope that you will help my sister in the way I tried to do, but couldn't," she whispered.

He pulled out his mobile and shot off a text to the head of his security. "She will be removed from your family's home within the hour and installed in the palace. Will that do?"

"Orion." And the way she said his name was like an ache. "I didn't come here to tell you that I was calling off our wedding. I came to give you those pictures, so that part would be ended. And with the full understanding that once my father's leverage over you was gone, you might be perfectly happy to see the back of me. I accept that."

Though he noted, with some satisfaction, that she sounded wretched. Not accepting.

"If you wish to leave me at the altar, Calista, you will have to do it yourself," he growled at her. "I will be there tomorrow in the Grand Cathedral, ready and waiting to make you my queen. All you need to do is show up. Or not."

She pushed against him, shaking her head.

"You can do so much better than me. You could have anyone. Why would you want the daughter—"

"I don't care who your father is," he told her, his face low, and his mouth against hers, like a vow. "I don't care who my father is, either. It's time for us to bury them, Calista. You and me, together. We will put them in the ground, one way or another, and we will find our way into our own future. A future that has nothing to do with either one of them."

She gazed up at him, looking caught somewhere between despair and hope, and so he kissed her.

Because words were only words, but this—

This was real.

This was them.

It had already changed both of them. So deeply that Orion doubted either one of them could ever go back to who they'd been before.

Good, a voice in him said. Smugly.

"I love you," Calista whispered, there against his mouth. And the words made his heart thud. "I tried so hard not to love you. I told myself I couldn't love anyone. But in the end, I thought of you and I emptied out my father's safe, and I ran straight here."

"Calista," he said, like her name was a song. He rested his forehead against hers. "Tomorrow you will be my queen. But I believe I have loved you from the first moment I saw you, standing out on the balcony with your eyes on the sea. I loved you then. And if you will let me, I will dedicate my life to loving you forever."

"I don't know if I believe in forever," she replied, tears pouring down her face. "But if you do, then I'll try. I'll dedicate my life to trying, and giving you every reason in the world to trust me. I promise."

"And I promise you, I will give you the same." His lips crooked into a smile. "And you know I am excellent at keeping promises."

"Just as you know I'm terrific at keeping my focus," she replied, the sparkle he loved so much returning to her gaze.

It felt like another song.

And then his mouth was on hers, she was wrapped around him, and he bore her down to the floor before the fire.

He kissed her and he kissed her, over and over, hardly able to believe that this was real.

"Orion…" she whispered.

He took his time, peeling her out of the sharp, sleek clothes that made her look so dangerous. Then he feasted upon her.

He took her breasts in his hands, tasting one hard nipple, then the other. She moaned, arching against him, and he wanted too much. He wanted everything.

Orion shrugged out of his own clothes, sighing with a kind of relief when her hands found the hard ridges of his abdomen, then moved lower to worship the hardest part of him.

Her eyes were wide with a kind of mute pleading as she shifted, moving lower so she could take him in her mouth.

A sweet promise. A wicked temptation.

A kind of vow, he thought, as she licked her way along the length of him as if tasting his heat was a sacred act all its own.

And when he could take no more, he pulled her up and astride him, settling her so he could feel the molten heat of her all over him, where her mouth had just been.

"You are mine," he told her, like a vow. "Always."

"Forever," she agreed, and then she impaled herself upon him.

And they both groaned with the pleasure of it. The slick, hot glory that was only theirs.

She moved her hips, an endless seduction. And together, they made vows to each other that would last a lifetime. With their bodies and their words. With the deep thrust and breathless retreat.

With the spiraling heights he took her to, his hands gripping her hips as he took control, lifting and lowering her. He watched her shake apart, flying over that cliff into a thousand bright pieces. He kept going, flipping her over and driving himself in deeper.

His first. His last. His only.

He waited until the fire in her burned anew, and only when she cried out his name again did he let himself go, following her over the edge of the world.

Later tonight they would burn to ash the bitter legacy her father had collected. They would render him even more toothless and dismissible than he already was this night.

Here before the fire, they were new.

Come the dawn, it would be Christmas Eve. He would make her his queen.

And he was His Majesty Orion Augustus Pax, King of Idylla, so he did exactly that— and then he set about loving her for the rest of his life, because she deserved no less.

And because she loved him right back.

Hard and true, fierce and faithful, until they were both so happy it was hard to remember that they had ever been anything else.

CHAPTER THIRTEEN

CALISTA MARRIED KING ORION OF IDYLLA in the Grand Cathedral with the whole of the kingdom watching.

The people poured into the cathedral itself. They lined the streets, though it was a blustery day, which everyone said felt appropriately Christmassy, with the holiday decorations lighting up the trees and every house in the land bright with celebratory candles.

Inside, she took Orion's hands. She gazed into his eyes and she said her vows.

Then she kissed him in front of the world and made it real.

And when he led her out of the cathedral again, she was a queen.

His queen.

Together, they sat in a carriage open to the elements, and though it was not warm, neither one of them felt the chill. The carriage led them up a winding road toward the palace, lined all the way with Christmas lights and cheering subjects.

And at the final ball of the Idyllian holiday season, always traditionally held in the palace, they celebrated their wedding—and more than that, their miraculous love for each other, where everyone could see it.

Feel it. Wonder at it, if they liked—or wonder why her parents weren't at the ceremony, which would no doubt be in all the papers the next day.

Calista found she couldn't care less. Melody was safe.

Her parents were the past.

Orion was the future.

This time, when Orion led her out onto the dance floor, he didn't pretend to be stern and austere. He smiled down at her in her Cinderella dress, until she thought that surely every person in the whole of the kingdom of Idylla could see that he was besotted.

But then, so was she, and she didn't care who saw it.

"My queen," he said formally, as he swept her into his arms. "Your Royal Highness."

"My love," she said in reply.

And they danced.

They danced and they danced, and they celebrated the love they'd almost lost, before finding it at the very last moment.

They danced. They celebrated. The king made a speech, and outside the crowds cheered them by name.

Most of what Calista would remember of this night was him. Her beautiful Orion, his eyes gleaming gold, as they claimed each other at last.

And when the clock struck midnight, it really was Christmas, at last.

Her king and her love—her husband—dispensed with tradition and tedious royal decorum. He swept her up into his arms to the delight of the crowd, and then he carried her up the grand staircase, heading for the family wing of the palace.

He didn't put her down when he'd climbed the stairs. Nor did turn toward her suite.

Instead, he carried her into the sprawling King's Suite.

"I have already moved your things," he told her sternly. "And I will tell you now, Calista, that I have no intention of maintaining separate lives. Or rooms. Or anything of the sort."

"Perish the thought, my liege," she said, smiling, with her head on his shoulder.

"It is clear to me that I am going to require access to my queen," he said, as he strode into a chamber with a bed raised high on a dais, with four posters soaring high, as befitted a king.

"You have all the access you like," she assured him. "As long as I can access the king in turn."

He laid her down on the bed, came down with her, and for a moment, they both smiled so wide, so bright, it was as if they created their own full moon there between them. To watch the one outside that hung there, for them, lighting up the sea.

"Merry Christmas, my love," Orion said.

"Merry Christmas," Calista replied.

And then, together, they set about unwrapping their gifts.

That night, each other.

And nine months later a red-faced, squalling crown prince.

Followed not long after by a fierce little princess.

And one more of each.

"For good luck," Orion liked to say, gathering their children in his arms and looking at her over their heads with those beautiful hazel eyes gone gold.

Calista knew they had no need of luck.

Because they had each other and that was better and sweeter than luck could ever be.

But to make sure, she loved him with all her heart, and let him love her the same way in return.

Forever and ever, and that was just the start.

* * * * *